Francesca stuck her spoon in the Triple Fudge Marshmallow Chunk. "Don't you wonder about her? I do. Because she's obviously a deep person. So I can't imagine all she cares about is teaching boring U.S. History to boring seventh graders. Especially in Blanton."

"Hey, Blanton's not so bad," I protested.

She ignored that. "You've seen those posters on her walls. She's traveled all over the world. So why is she wasting her life *here*? Unless," she added dramatically, "she has some dark, romantic secret."

"Like what?"

She leaned forward, breathing chocolate in my face. "I'll tell you, but you can't tell anyone else."

OTHER BOOKS BY BARBARA DEE

JUST ANOTHER DAY IN MY INSANELY REAL LIFE

SOLVING ZOE

this is me from now on

BARBARA DEE

little M!X

Aladdin M!X

New York   London   Toronto   Sydney

m!x

ALADDIN M!X
Simon & Schuster Children's Publishing Division
1230 Avenue of the Americas, New York, NY 10020
First Aladdin M!X edition April 2010
Copyright © 2010 by Barbara Dee
All rights reserved, including the right of reproduction
in whole or in part in any form.
ALADDIN is a trademark of Simon & Schuster, Inc., and related logo
is a registered trademark of Simon & Schuster, Inc.
ALADDIN M!X and related logo are registered trademarks
of Simon & Schuster, Inc.
For information about special discounts for bulk purchases,
please contact Simon & Schuster Special Sales at
1-866-506-1949 or business@simonandschuster.com.
The Simon & Schuster Speakers Bureau can bring authors to your
live event. For more information or to book an event contact
the Simon & Schuster Speakers Bureau at 1-866-248-3049
or visit our website at www.simonspeakers.com.
Designed by Ann Zeak
The text of this book was set in Lomba Book.
Manufactured in the United States of America
0113 OFF
4 6 8 10 9 7 5 3
Library of Congress Control Number 2009928150
ISBN 978-1-4169-9414-5
ISBN 978-1-4169-9923-2 (eBook)

For Chris, with love

Acknowledgments

Heartfelt thanks to my agent, Jill Grinberg, for taking such good care of this book right from the beginning. A majillion thank-yous to my editor, Liesa Abrams, for connecting so strongly with the characters and with me. I'm incredibly lucky to be working with you both.

Thanks also to Karen Wojtyla for putting me on the right track with the first draft, and to Frances O'Roark Dowell for making sure I didn't derail. Helen Silberblatt, thanks so much for all your freelance publicizing—but really for the precious gift of your friendship.

Infinite gratitude to my husband, Chris, for reading every word of every draft, and for making every word possible.

As always, thanks to my mom and dad for endless love and support. And to Alex, Josh, and Lizzy, thanks for . . . aw shucks, just being you.

chapter 1

Sometimes your life just needs a little jolt.

That's what Francesca told me once, and she was right. I mean, she was wrong about practically everything, but she was right about that. Because the more I think about it, the more I look back at all the chaos that happened last fall, it's almost like she rescued me.

Okay, okay. I know that sounds incredibly melodramatic. And I know that mainly she messed things up. Really, really badly, in fact.

But let me put it this way: The Thursday late last summer when I first met Francesca Pattison is the last boring day I can remember. I'd spent most of the morning Mother's

Helping and most of the afternoon in my best friend Lily's bedroom, eating Pringles (which I didn't even like) and taking personality quizzes from this enormous stack of magazines that Lily had borrowed from her cousin in New Jersey. "Was I Due for a Hot New Makeover?" Well, maybe. Maybe not. "Was I You Ready for a Steady?" Definitely no. Not even close.

The room was totally sweltering, because Lily's dad didn't believe in air-conditioning ("for the environment," he said, but to be honest I think he was just cheap). And the rotating fan was making this *fwish-fwish-fwish* noise that was starting to make me woozy.

Nisha, my other best friend, opened a magazine. "Here's one, Evie," she said. 'Are You Crushed by a Crush?'"

"Did that one," I said, yawning.

"And are you?"

"What? Of course not."

"What about your crush on Zane?" Lily asked, smiling.

"Gah. I don't even know if I *like* him anymore."

"Oh, right," Nisha said. "We totally believe you, Evie. So how about this one: 'Feel Bad About That Bod?'"

"Also did," I said. "And I happen to feel great about my bod. In fact, I love my bod, I worship my bod."

Nisha rolled her eyes. She'd been bathing suit shopping with me a million times that summer, so she knew exactly how I felt about my flat chest and bony elbows. Not to mention my blobby nose and used-to-be-blonder hair. "What about 'Cheat Sheet: Rate Your Talent for Trickery.'"

"Actually, I think I missed that one. Ask me it, okay?"

Nisha read out loud: "'You're committed to Saturday night with your BFFs, but the new hottie asks you to the movies. You (a) ask the hottie if your BFFs can join you; (b) tell your BFFs your cousin's in town; (c) call your BFFs at the last minute and say you've come down with the flu—'"

She stopped. "Eww, this is disgusting. I'd *hate* any girl who acted like this."

"Me too," Lily said. She leaned across my legs and tickled her smelly old dog, Jimmy, whose giant paws were twitching in his sleep. "So two-faced."

"But what's wrong with 'a'?" I asked curiously.

"What's *wrong* with it?" Nisha repeated. "Evie, 'a' would be totally wimping out on your friends."

"Even if they were invited along?"

"They wouldn't want to be 'invited along.' You were supposed to be going out with *them*. See the word 'committed'?"

"Hey, don't attack *me*, Nisha. I'm just saying—"

"You're saying some boy would be more important than your best friends since preschool? Well, thanks a lot, Evie. At least we know where we'd stand." Nisha's black eyes flashed, the way they do whenever she's mad. But then all of a sudden she grinned at me. "Just kidding," she said, sticking out her tongue.

So Lily threw a magazine at her.

I stood up then and brushed off the Pringle bits that were sticking to my legs. "Okay, you guys. This has been oodles of fun, but I think I'm going home now."

"But it's only three thirty," Lily protested.

"Yeah, but I'm tired. And summer's almost over, and we're just sitting here wasting time with these old magazines."

Lily's eyes looked hurt. "So what would you rather be doing?"

"I don't know," I admitted. "Something crazy and different. And fun."

Nisha closed her magazine. "You know what, Evie? I think the heat's melting your brain. Why don't you take a long, cold shower, and tomorrow we'll go buy school supplies."

"*School supplies?* Nisha, that's not my idea of—"

"And afterward we'll go bungee jumping. And hot-air ballooning."

Lily laughed. "Don't forget white-water rafting."

"Okay, stop," I said. "Really."

"And then we'll go visit Zane," Nisha added. She winked at Lily like it was all decided.

I groaned at that. You have to understand that I loved my friends, even though they knew exactly how to annoy me. Nisha was an expert in teasing and also organizing my life; Lily was an expert in calming me down, even when I didn't *want* to be calmed down. They also knew how to make me laugh and keep me sane, but right now what I really needed was to get out of that sweaty bedroom.

So I left.

The second I was outside on the baking asphalt, I was thinking: *Well, Evie, that was smart.* In a few days the three of us would be in total Back-to-School mode, like summer never even happened. I'd left Lily's to do what? Take a ten-minute shower? And *then* what was supposed to happen the whole rest of the afternoon?

At least my own house was freezingly air-conditioned. As soon as I opened the front door, I took a deep breath of that dead-cold air and felt the sweat ice up on my legs. Then

I took off my flip-flops and walked into the living room, which was always the nippiest room in the house.

Francesca Pattison was sitting in what Mom calls the loveseat. I didn't really focus on her at first—I was too busy staring at her aunt Samantha. It was one of the few times I'd seen Samantha Pattison in daylight. Mostly my sister and I had just peeked at her late at night slamming the door of a black BMW convertible, and then clattering up her driveway in noisy, high-heeled shoes. None of us could figure out why a thirty-fivish woman with no kids and an obviously amazing social life would choose to live in our nice but extremely nonamazing subdivision. Samantha Pattison was something to talk about when we needed a topic at the dinner table.

And now here she was sipping Diet Snapple with my mom, looking normal and suburban in a yellow flowered sundress and sandals. "So grateful," I heard her saying as I plopped into a squishy armchair.

"Hi, honey. You remember our neighbor, Ms. Pattison?" Mom said, giving me a look.

"Oh, sure," I lied, because how could I remember someone I'd never even officially met? "Hi."

"And this is her niece Francesca." Mom turned to where

Francesca was sitting, but she wasn't there anymore. Now she was standing by our big bookshelf, pulling down book after book.

The first thing I thought about her was: *Omigod. That girl is a giant. Is she taller than Dad? I think she is.*

"Your books are so BRILLIANT," she was practically shouting. "*Wuthering Heights*—I *love* this book! It's the most gorgeous book ever written. Can I borrow it?"

"We can borrow books from the Blanton Library," her aunt Samantha said. "Say hello to Eva."

"Evie," I said automatically.

"Francesca is entering seventh grade too," Mom said, smiling. "She's a sort of transfer student."

"Oh, really? From where?" I asked.

"The depths of hell," Francesca answered.

Samantha Pattison giggled, rattling her ice cubes. "You don't mean that, sugarpie."

"Oh yes I do."

"Why? What was wrong with your old school?" I asked.

"Everything," Francesca said, looking right at me as if she were confessing some top secret. "They tried to suppress my spirit, but of course they failed miserably."

The second thing I thought was: *Whoa. That girl looks incredible. I wish my hair was long and all wavy like that, and my eyes were that smoky sort of green. And I bet SHE doesn't have trouble finding a bathing suit!* The third thing was: *On the other hand, she's crazy.*

"Evie, honey," Mom said, "why don't you get yourself some lemonade, and then maybe you could take Francesca over to see Blanton Middle."

"You mean right now?"

"Oh, that's not necessary, Mrs. Webber," said Francesca. "I prefer not to think about school. It's not for ages, anyway."

Mom smiled. "Actually, it's less than a week away. In Blanton we start school in late August."

"Then we still have eons," Francesca answered cheerfully. "But I'd absolutely love a walk, Evie, if you really wouldn't mind."

"I wouldn't mind," I said, looking helplessly at Mom. "It's just incredibly hot out there."

"That's all right," Francesca said. "I've been living in Saudi Arabia. I'm used to extreme temperatures."

"Francesca's dad is in the oil business," Samantha Pattison explained.

"Oh." I knew I was supposed to be impressed by that, but

I didn't even know what "the oil business" meant, exactly. I looked at Francesca. "You want some lemonade too?"

"No thanks," she said. "I've already had three absolutely scrumptious glasses."

Okaaaay, I thought. I went into the kitchen and got myself a glass of ice cubes surrounded by lemonade. Grace, my school-aholic big sister, was sitting at the dining room table hunched over a book called *Acing the SAT.* She filled in a test bubble and looked up at me, grinning. "Samantha Pattison," she said.

"I know. In broad daylight."

"With her niece."

"I know. Did you meet her? She seems—"

"Not now," murmured Grace, raising her eyebrows.

"Are you ready, Evie?" someone said from behind me. Francesca clomped into the dining room. That's when I noticed she was wearing a normal-looking outfit (purple tank top, green shorts) but also these pointy-toed, sparkly blue stilettos with, like, four-inch super-skinny heels.

I swear, when I saw those shoes I practically choked on an ice cube. Because I'd never seen anything like them in my entire life; I had no idea what I was supposed to think about them. It was like a quiz from one of Lily's magazines:

What's your take on Francesca's shoes?

(a) Soooo tacky—*What was she thinking?*

(b) Soooo babyish—*Is she channeling Cinderella?*

(c) Soooo weird—*Do they wear those things on Neptune?*

(d) Soooo hot—*I wonder if they'd fit me!*

And here's the funny part: I realized I was thinking all four things at the same time. So maybe the right answer was (e) All of the above. Even if that wasn't a choice.

Now Francesca clomped over to Grace. "What are you doing?" she asked, trying to read upside down.

"Studying for the SAT," Grace answered.

"But it's only August. Why worry about some bloody awful test before school even starts?"

Grace smiled in this superior way she has. "Well, I'm a senior in high school. Going to be. And if I want to go to a good college, I need to take the SAT this fall."

"How *sad*," said Francesca. "That's why I absolutely refuse to go to college, among other reasons. Well, don't let us distract you." Then her face brightened. "Unless you'd like to come with us? We're going for a nice long walk."

"That's okay," Grace said, catching my eye. "Have fun,

you two." She picked up a pencil and flipped a page in her SAT book, pretending not to laugh.

I squinted at Francesca. Even outside in the glaring sunshine she looked fantastic: her skin was a golden tan, and her hair was the color of Kraft Caramels. "So where do you want to go?" I asked, my teeth skidding on the last little slivers of ice cubes.

"Oh, you decide," Francesca said happily. "You're the expert."

"I am?"

"Well, you live here, don't you? Where do you go when you want to have fun?"

"I don't know. The mall, probably. When someone's mom can drive us."

She made a face. "Where else?"

"The park. The movies. The stores on Elm."

"Blah. Boring."

"The ice cream place—"

"Ooh, ice cream," she said, clapping her hands. "What a genius idea. Is it far?"

"Sort of. Half a mile, maybe."

"Oh, that's nothing. I love to walk."

I looked at her feet. "Even in those shoes? They don't look very comfortable."

"Oh, they're not. They're bloody torture, actually. But they're so epically gorgeous, don't you think?" She took off her left shoe. I could see the side of her foot near her big toe looked pink and peely. She rubbed it, then put the shoe right back on and beamed at me. "Besides, if Mother Darling saw me wearing them, she'd go berserk. So who cares about stupid blisters."

I didn't know what to say to that; it never occurred to me to *want* my mom to go berserk. The truth is, Mom went berserk all the time, over things like unwashed dishes and unmade beds, and I didn't exactly find it entertaining. And why did Francesca just call her own mom 'Mother Darling'? She talked really, really strangely, like everything she said was in quotation marks or something.

We walked long blocks without saying very much. The air was so hot, it was almost chewy, and I could feel the sweat trickling down my armpits, even though this morning I'd snuck some of Grace's powder-fresh deodorant. Francesca was definitely limping by now. Once or twice I saw her stop and rub her foot, but she never complained or took her shoe off again. Finally she pointed across the street. "Is that the ice cream place, Evie? It looks like heaven."

"I wouldn't go that far," I said. "But I really like their chocolate chip."

She wiped her forehead. "Yum, chocolate chip. My absolute favorite."

We crossed the street and went inside. Oh, I should tell you that I Scream for Ice Cream (I know, I know: dumb name) was owned by Zane's dad, and Zane helped out there sometimes. Today was one of those days, probably because the place was packed with sticky first graders off the camp bus and moms sick of dieting all summer to fit into bathing suits and middle schoolers in denial about the end of vacation.

We got in line. As soon as we did, the door opened again, and two girls I knew from school walked in: Kayla and Gaby. Definitely cooler-than-me types, but I'd say lower-medium-nice.

"Hey, Evie," said Kayla, finger-combing her fakely high-lighted long brown hair. "What Team are you on? Hard or Easy?"

"I don't know. I haven't read my letter yet." This was true; I'd gotten my Seventh-Grade Team Assignment Letter last week, but I'd just stuffed it into my desk drawer.

Kayla smiled like she didn't believe me. "We're both on Hard. What about Nisha and Lily?"

"Hard," I said. "Like always."

"Poor them," Gaby commented. "Hard has Espee."

I nodded. Oh yes, I knew all about the Espee business. When my sister, Grace, took seventh-grade U.S. History, all she did—I mean literally, ALL SHE DID—was research and write bibliographies, sometimes until two in the morning. Her social life basically ended that year; the only thing she cared about was satisfying this insatiable monster she referred to as SP. I was, like, seven years old then, so I thought "SP" stood for something too horrible to call a teacher out loud, like Scary Person or Sour Pickle. Finally I asked Grace what SP meant, and she said, "Stephanie Pierce. She signs everything SP, so that's what we call her." "To her *face*?" I'd asked. "Of course not," Grace had said, hooting at my stupidity. "She'd vaporize you."

Francesca, who I *could* have introduced at that point, was standing on her tippy-toes, even though she was nearly six feet tall with those all-of-the-above shoes. "What does that sign say?" she asked too loudly. "Mochaccino Supremo? What's that?" And then she turned around and grinned at me. "Deeply gorgeous boy. Behind the counter."

In back of me, Gaby started giggling. I've always hated the way she sounded when she laughed, kind of like a car alarm.

"That's Zane," Kayla announced. "He's in eighth grade."

"Zane," Francesca repeated still-too-loudly. "What an odd name." Then she stared at me with her huge, smoky green eyes. "You're in love with him, Evie, aren't you?"

"What?"

"I'm psychic about these things. I should have warned you."

"Yes? Next in line?" Zane called out.

"Oops, my turn!" Francesca walked right up to Zane, gave him a dazzling smile, and asked, "So, Zane, what do you recommend?"

I could have died. What did he *recommend*? Gah. Didn't she even know how to order ice cream like a normal human being? I could hear Gaby and Kayla laughing, maybe about Francesca, maybe about me. And then I saw Zane hand Francesca a tiny plastic spoon and one of those little paper cups they used for free samples.

Francesca took a spoonful of whatever-it-was. "Ooh, lovely," she said. She pointed to some other kind of ice cream in the case. "What's that?"

"Triple Fudge Marshmallow Chunk. Try it," said Zane, handing her another paper cup.

"Yumyumyum," said Francesca when she'd taken a bite. "What's that?"

He read the label upside down. "Um, Golden Brownie with Caramel Fudge Ripple."

Francesca clutched her chest like she was having a heart attack.

So Zane handed her another free sample.

"Bliss," Francesca said. "I've never tasted anything so epically delish!"

"Aaaa, come on, dude, we're waiting here," snarled some high-school-looking boy three customers behind me.

"Be right with you," Zane answered. But he just kept handing Francesca free sample after free sample. And Francesca just kept pointing at the ice cream freezer and saying "lovely" and "yummy" and "Ooh, what's that?" Finally a grouchy mom with one of those sticky camp kids called out, "Excuse me, but is this line ever *moving*?" And then the sticky camp kid yelled at her, "Mommy, you said I could have ice cream *NOW*!"

I felt a jabbing poke on my shoulder.

"Hey, Evie, aren't you with that girl?" Kayla was asking.

"Who?"

She tilted her highlights toward Francesca. "*Her.* The one eating up half the freezer."

"Her name is Francesca," I said. I was about to add, "I don't even know her," but I stopped myself. After all, they'd heard her call me Evie; they'd almost definitely also heard about her psychic powers.

Suddenly, Sticky Camp Kid started screaming his head off, and Grouchy Mom was telling him, "You'll get your ice cream in TWO MORE MINUTES, buddy," like it was a threat aimed right at Zane, and I thought: *Okay. If I don't do something NOW, Francesca Pattison is going to start a riot in here. Everyone in this line is going to leap into that freezer and start scooping ice cream with their bare hands. And maybe throwing it at her like snowballs.* And even though walking over to Francesca was like posting on YouTube that we had some kind of official connection, at this point I really didn't think I had too much of a choice.

So I went over to her. She was pointing at a melty-looking tub of Rainbow Cotton Candy. "Ooh, *that* looks interesting," she was commenting to Zane. Then she noticed me. "Have you ever tried that flavor, Evie?"

"Not really. But I bet it's great." I added under my breath, "Just order something, Francesca. Okay?"

"Are you all right?" she asked me, scrunching up her forehead like she was worried about my health.

"Yes! Just *please, please* hurry up."

"Oh, sure." She put her tiny paper cup and her plastic spoon on the counter, smiled at Zane, and said, "It's all spectacular, Zane. But I'm afraid I'm absolutely stuffed. I'll have to come back for a cone some other time."

He blinked his gold-hazel eyes. "You mean you're not buying anything?"

"Oh, *no* thank you. But Evie will, I think."

We watched her clomp to the door.

"I'll have a chocolate chip cone," I said quickly. "Single scoop, please."

When Zane handed it to me, our knuckles sort of banged into each other, and it shocked me just how freezing his hand was. I mean, he was scooping ice cream all day; *of course* his hand would be icy cold. But it made me feel weird, like I wanted to run home and knit him some gloves. And the crazy thing is, I don't even knit.

So instead I reached into my pocket and gave him every bit of money I had—four dollars and fifty-three cents.

"That's for Francesca too," I said. Then brilliantly I added, "Uh, sorry, Zane."

"No problem," he muttered. I watched him stuff the money in the register without even counting it. Then he did this cool little head-jerk to toss his long, wavy bangs out of his face. "Next?"

"Bye, Evie, see you at school!" Gaby called out.

"What school?" I answered. I grabbed a fistful of napkins and walked out into the scorching heat.

Francesca was standing right in front of the door, shading her eyes. "What kind did you get? Chocolate chip? I adore that flavor. It's my absolute favorite!"

"You said that before." Already it was starting to drip down the sides of my cone, so I licked it fast. "Then why didn't you get any?"

"Because . . . well, chocolate chip is always exactly the same." She did that heart-clutching thing again. "And there were so many other flavors. And they all looked so scrumptious. Evie, don't you ever get *utterly bored*—"

"No." I wrapped a napkin around the soggy cone. "The thing is, Francesca, I'm pretty sure Zane thought you'd pick a flavor. Eventually. And then pay him for it."

She looked shocked. "Oh, I would have. But of course I couldn't."

"Why not?"

"Because I don't have any money." She pulled out her shorts pockets. They were totally empty. "See?" she said, smiling sweetly.

Okay. Okay. I had *no idea* what I was supposed to say to that. Because what did she think she was doing just now? Ice cream research? And why hadn't she just told me that on the way over? I'd have loaned her some money; I'd pretty much paid for her anyway. I mean, I didn't even know what to *think* about a person who could act the way she just had.

And in front of so many people. Including people I knew. People I'd be going to school with in just a few more days.

Gah. It was just too horrible. And embarrassing. And weird. So for the entire walk home I tried really, really hard to tune her out. She was going on and on about some gelato place she went to once in Rome or something, but I just made myself think about Zane, and whether or not he blamed *me,* and also how much longer I could go without opening my Team Letter. And I concentrated extremely hard on my lopsided ice cream cone, trying to catch the drips before they splattered on the sidewalk.

chapter 2

hen I walked into the kitchen, Mom was on the phone, sitting in front of a bunch of real estate papers.

"Shirt," she whispered, pointing to my lemon-yellow tank top. I looked: Right in the middle of my chest was a melted chocolate chip smear, which probably wouldn't even come out in the wash. And this was my best tank too, the only one that made me feel as if I had a right to wear a bra.

"Is that chocolate?" Mom asked in a normal voice, frowning at my chest. "So close to supper?"

"I know, Mom. But I didn't have a choice. Francesca insisted—"

"Go clean up," she ordered. "Dad's on his way home and we'll be eating at six thirty." Suddenly her face got all delightful, the way she always looks when she's on the phone with her clients. "Caroline? Great news. I think we finally have an offer!"

I went upstairs to my room, took off my sweaty, smeary tank top, and put on this cute but way-too-enormous San Diego Zoo T-shirt Lily brought me back when she visited her mom a few months ago. Then I opened my desk drawer. Right on top of my Team Letter was the choker I'd bought last week at the mall: a tiny chunk of real amber on a black silk cord.

"You're *buying* that?" Nisha had screeched at me while we were standing at the cash register. "That's how you're blowing your entire Mother's Helper money?"

"It's beautiful," I'd answered. "Besides, I earned it. You know how many times this summer I had to play Candy Land with Ashley Scavullo?" She was four years old; basically her mom was paying me to come over in the mornings so she could talk on the phone.

Nisha grabbed the necklace out of my hand and stared at it. Then she pushed it back at me. "Evie. Listen to me carefully. It has a *bug* in it."

"That's because it's real amber," I told her. "It's supposed to be that way."

She made a face. "Supposed?"

"It's a mosquito fossil. It could be, like, a billion years old."

"Uh-huh," she replied. "Cute. And would you wear some gross woolly mammoth tusk around your neck too?"

Now I held up the necklace to my desk lamp. I examined the floating mosquito, which actually *was* kind of gross, I had to admit. But the amber around it reminded me of Zane's eyes in a certain kind of light, so it was worth every single penny. I fastened the silk cord around my neck and snuck into the bathroom to look at myself. The amber glowed; amazingly, so did I. For the first time all day I felt happy and calm and unweird.

Then I took off the necklace and opened my Team Letter. Fast.

Dear Eva J. Webber,

Welcome to Team F ("THE HARD TEAM"). For the next ten months, your life (to the extent you'll have one) will be a total nightmare. We can't wait to begin! Here is a ridiculously specific list of

this is me from now on

miscellaneous junk you'll probably never use but
will need to buy anyway—

Okay, so maybe that's not what it actually said. But I knew
what it meant: Of the two academic teams for seventh grade,
I was placed on the tougher one, the one that got assigned
all the work, the one that had Espee for U.S. History. I tried
not to freak out too badly, even though under Stephanie
Pierce's name it said we needed to buy ten spiral notebooks.
(TEN SPIRAL NOTEBOOKS? *TEN???*) Plus, we needed ten
packs of index cards, and twelve different folders in twelve
different colors. As soon as I read all that, I speed-dialed
Lily so she could try to calm me down. But her line was
busy, so then I called Nisha. First she screamed into her cell
when I told her I was on the Hard Team. And then even *she*
admitted: Just from the supplies list alone, you could tell
this was going to be a nightmare year in U.S. History.

And now that I'd finally opened the Team Letter, summer was officially over. Which meant that the Espee nightmare had already begun.

Around nine the next morning, Nisha's mom drove up to
take us to Staples. I knew they were here because Nisha
started beeping the horn.

"Not so loud," I muttered to Nisha as soon as I got into the car. "Hi, Mrs. Guptil."

"Good morning, Evie," Mrs. Guptil said. "I told Nisha not to beep, but you know she never, never listens."

"Sorry," Nisha said. "Did I just wake your entire family, Evie?"

Mrs. Guptil turned around. "That's exactly what I told her: *You'll wake the entire family.* And it's Saturday; Evie's parents work very hard all week and need to sleep as late as possible."

I smiled. "Actually, they've been up for hours. I just meant, don't wake the neighbors."

Nisha raised her eyebrows at me. "Really? Why not?"

"No reason. I'll tell you later."

She shrugged. But I was positive she knew what I was thinking; I mean, we'd talked about it a million times. Nisha's mom was incredibly nice to be taking us out for school supplies, but you had to watch every single word you said in front of her, because she gossiped like crazy. (Actually, the truth was, she just about never stopped *talking*.) That was definitely the bad side of hanging out at Nisha's, but of course, everybody's house had Pros and Cons. Even mine, I told myself, although right then the only Pro I could think of was Freezing Air Conditioning.

And now we were driving up to Lily's house, which was the farthest away from town (definitely a Con). Mrs. Guptil was going on and on about how unfair it was that we had to buy our own pencils, when I noticed Lily standing in her driveway with her dog, Jimmy. I poked Nisha.

Lily came running up to the car. "Is it okay if I bring Jimmy? His stomach is a little funny, and I really don't want to leave him alone."

"Lily, my darling," said Mrs. Guptil, "I'm really very sorry, but I can't have that stinky old dog in my car." She made a bad-smell face and waved her hand in front of her nose.

"Oh, I thought of that," Lily said quickly. She reached into her shoulder bag and pulled out a travel-size bottle of spray detangler. Then, before anybody could stop her, she sprayed Jimmy's butt.

"Omigod, I can't believe you did that!" Nisha cried. She looked at me in shock, and then we both started laughing.

"See?" Lily said to Mrs. Guptil. "Now Jimmy smells like—what's it called? Jasmine Orange Blossom. Isn't that so much better?" She opened the car door, and Jimmy hopped in beside her, smelling so jasminey and orange blossomy, he made my eyes tear.

Mrs. Guptil fanned the car air, but I could see in the rearview mirror that she was smiling. She always spoiled Lily, probably because Lily's parents were divorced and Lily hardly ever saw her mother. That was another nice thing about Mrs. Guptil, I had to admit.

About ten minutes later we were at Staples. The parking lot was mobbed, not surprising for the Saturday before school. Lily gave a few private instructions to Jimmy, who she left curled up on her car seat with a still-flower-smelling butt and a half-eaten chew toy. Then we grabbed a shopping cart and did our annual mad dash through the store, yanking supplies off the shelves and tossing them into the cart while Mrs. Guptil checked things off the Team F Supplies List and scolded us for making her lose track.

Aisle Six, Notebooks & Binders, was where I nearly crashed into Francesca. She was standing there with a completely empty shopping cart, studying her supplies list as if it were some kind of treasure map. Today she was wearing a halter sundress the color of those traffic cones you see on the highway, and gold chandelier earrings like the kind you wear to the Oscars, but at least she was wearing normal-looking flip-flops. Well, okay, semi-normal: They had ginormous patent-leather daisies on the toe-dividers.

She was just about to turn in my direction when Samantha Pattison came racing down the aisle with a huge stack of loose-leaf paper.

"Found it," she sang out. "Aisle Three, next to Index Cards. Oh, look, sugarpie, is that our neighbor Evie?"

"Hi, Ms. Pattison," I called politely. "Hi, Francesca."

Francesca looked up, obviously thrilled to see me. "Oh, Evie. Did your plans fall through?"

"What plans?"

"Your mother said you had plans today. With old friends."

I felt myself blushing. "Right. No, we ended up here. Like everybody else. So do you need any help?"

She looked surprised. "With what?"

"Your supplies list. I know it probably looks sort of overwhelming."

"Oh, *no* thanks—I've decided not to buy all that stuff. I'm really fine with just paper and pens."

"Actually, you aren't." I tried to catch Samantha Pattison's eye as she inspected the binders. "They're incredibly strict about supplies."

Francesca laughed loudly, as if I'd just said something hilarious. "Oh, help, I'm absolutely terrified. What do you think will happen—I'll get arrested by the Spiral Notebook Police?"

"It's not a joke, Francesca." Suddenly something occurred to me. "Okay if I see your list?"

She handed me her Team Letter. WELCOME TO TEAM F, it said. FOR THE NEXT TEN MONTHS—

I smiled vaguely and handed it back.

Just then Nisha came running over. "There you are," she said, panting. "I *might* have just seen Zane in Aisle Five, Mom's going completely nuts, and Lily thought she heard barking, so she went back to the car." She suddenly realized I'd been talking to Francesca. "Hi, I'm Nisha," she said, smiling. "Evie sucks at introductions."

"This is Francesca," I said, giving Nisha a look. "She's on Team F and she's also my *neighbor.*"

The word "neighbor" must have rung a bell, because Nisha blinked at me. "Well, nice to meet you, Francesca. I'm sure I'll see you around. Evie, we have, like, two minutes before Mom totally loses it."

"Okay," I said loudly. "We'd better find those Post-its, then. See you, Francesca."

Francesca gave us a dazzling smile, which for some reason made me feel guilty again, and we ran off.

"Why were you so weird just now?" Nisha asked as she grabbed a bunch of Post-its.

I gave her the sound bite of the whole ice cream store disaster. "And now she's standing in the middle of Staples refusing to buy school supplies. Does that even seem normal to you?"

"Maybe she's just cheap."

"She couldn't be. Her family's in the oil business."

"You mean like cooking oil?"

"No. I think like *oil* oil." I checked behind us to make sure she wasn't following. And also that Zane wasn't anywhere nearby. "That's why I didn't want you to beep before: so I wouldn't have to deal with her today."

"Well, anyway, she's not your problem," Nisha said distractedly. "Try not to obsess about her, okay? Look, there's Mom."

Mrs. Guptil was scolding some poor stock boy about the way they'd arranged the packs of subject dividers. We managed to drag her away and pay for our stuff, then cram it all into the car on the seat next to Jimmy. I couldn't help noticing he smelled even more like Jasmine Orange Blossom than before. Lily denied it, but I'm pretty positive she'd detangled his butt for the ride home. Anyway, I unrolled my window as far down as I could so at least my supplies wouldn't also stink for the entire school year.

That night, the second we sat down to dinner, the kitchen doorbell rang. And rang and rang, like there was some kind of big, scary emergency. My parents have a strict no-phone-calls-during-dinner policy, but doorbell ringing was different. I mean, you couldn't just sit there munching your broccoli while the whole house was vibrating.

So without even excusing myself, I got up from the table and opened the kitchen door.

It was Francesca. She was wearing one of those tacky Hawaiian shirts with grapefruit-size pink and yellow flowers, and also the gold chandelier earrings she'd had on at Staples. And she was holding an enormous red box that said, I SCREAM FOR ICE CREAM!

"Here," she said, handing it to me. "This is for yesterday at the ice cream place. I decided I desperately needed to apologize."

"No, you didn't," I said. Then I just stood there stupidly, holding the freezing, heavy box.

She tapped on the lid with a longish, chipped pink fingernail. "Well? Aren't you going to open it?"

So I opened it.

Inside was a gigantic white ice cream cake, the kind you get when you're five years old and have one of those mega-birthday parties where you invite the whole class. It had blue rosebuds with neon green leaves, and on the sides were those tiny bits of rainbow candy that look like confetti.

And on top, in swirly purple icing, it said, BON VOYAGE, LOIS & DAVE.

"Uh, thank you," I said slowly. "It looks delicious. But who are Lois and Dave?"

She laughed. "Nobody. I made them up. There wasn't room for 'Sorry I acted like such a greedy pig yesterday.'"

"You didn't—"

"Don't lie, Evie. You know that's exactly what you were thinking, so why not just admit it?"

"Okay. You kind of did, actually." I waited to feel proud of myself for being honest. When nothing happened, I added brilliantly, "Whoa. That is definitely a very large cake."

"I know; isn't it fantastic? And it has all the best flavors, but I can't remember their names. Anyway, I paid in cash, so all is forgiven."

"You mean with Zane?" I caught my breath. "How do you know that?"

"Relax, Evie. I could just tell. I even bought myself a *huge* scoop of chocolate chip. And you're right, it was deeply scrumptious."

I exhaled. Zane wasn't angry at her, which meant he wasn't angry at me. Well, that was certainly a major relief.

Francesca was beaming. "So. Aren't you going to have an enormous slice before it all melts?"

"It's six thirty," I answered. "We're just having dinner. I can't eat dessert before I finish dinner."

Then her smile flickered, the way lights do when there's a thunderstorm the next town over. And suddenly I found myself thinking, *Oh, Evie. Why can't you be nicer to her? She apologized, didn't she? Plus, she brought you this* cake.

Just then, Mom came into the kitchen. "Hi, Francesca," she said, her junk-food-detector automatically on High Alert. "Oh boy, what a beautiful cake. What does it say? 'Bon voyage—'"

"Lois and Dave," Francesca said helpfully. "Very old and dear friends of Aunt Sam's. They were shipping out for the Greek Isles, so they gave it to us. And since we're just about to take off too, we thought we'd share it with you." She smiled sweetly at Mom.

"How generous," Mom said, giving me a look. I knew

exactly what she wanted: I was supposed to say, *Oh yes, Francesca, how generous*. But I couldn't, because right at that moment I was too busy trying to read Francesca's eyes. Old and dear friends of Aunt Sam's? *What?* Just, like, thirty seconds ago she'd said that she'd "made up" Lois and Dave. And also paid Zane "in cash." She had the box from Zane's store, which meant she'd obviously bought the cake there. But then why would she lie to Mom about her aunt's "friends"? And the Greek Isles? What was even the point?

Mom opened the freezer and somehow stuffed in the cake without squishing the box. "Would you like to join us for dinner?" she was asking Francesca. "We're just now sitting down to veggie burgers."

Francesca held up her hand. "Oh, *no* thanks, Mrs. Webber. Aunt Sam and I are actually heading out the door. I promised I'd drop off the cake and then dash, and I'm interrupting your dinner, I can tell. Anyway, see you at school, Evie. In five days!"

"Four," I corrected her, watching from the kitchen window as she hopped into the black convertible and sped off.

chapter 3

The next three days flew by, but I'm not sure where they went. It was strange how I never once saw Francesca. Not that I wanted to, especially. But Mom insisted I ring her doorbell a couple of times to thank her for the Lois & Dave cake. She even suggested ("and this is just a *suggestion*," she said) that I invite her over to have some, since it was taking up so much room in our freezer.

But nobody ever answered their door, and I could see the mail starting to spill out of Samantha Pattison's mailbox. Then I remembered Francesca saying she and her aunt were just about to "take off" somewhere. I wondered where: back to Saudi Arabia? No; that was too big a trip if Francesca was going to make it back for the first day of school. But of course she'd thought school started in five days, not four, so maybe she didn't even *care* about showing up on time. Maybe going to Morning Homeroom and getting her schedule and all that other First Day of School stuff would be "suppressing her spirit," or whatever she'd called it. Maybe, I thought, she'd left Blanton Middle before she'd even started it.

And then all of a sudden, the night before school, she was back. Grace and I were just finishing up the dinner dishes when I heard a car screech up her driveway. So I peeked out the kitchen window and saw Francesca and Samantha getting out of the convertible, carrying a bunch of grocery bags and laughing their heads off.

"Just in time," commented Grace. "I thought we'd never seen them again."

"You thought they'd moved?" I asked.

"Fled," she answered as Samantha took a huge mosquito-zapper out of the trunk of her car.

That night just as I was pulling up my pj bottoms, I realized Grace was standing in my room. "How can you possibly sleep with all this noise?" she muttered.

"What noise?"

"You don't hear anything? God, Evie, you must be going deaf."

I followed her down the hall to her bedroom, which was thumping with some kind of horrible eighties-sounding music, plus the sound of people laughing like they were at the most fun party ever. Grace yanked open her lavender tie-dyed curtains and we both stared out. You couldn't see very much from that angle, but I could just make out Samantha's back deck, and about twenty incredibly gorgeous grown-ups (male and female) dancing, drinking, talking, and obviously having a fabulous time. And in the corner of the deck was Francesca, leaning against the railing and eating what looked like an enormous sandwich.

Grace glared. "I can't *believe* how inconsiderate this is. Doesn't Samantha Pattison read the school calendar?"

"Why should she?"

"Well, theoretically Francesca's going to school in the morning, right? Somebody should do something."

"Like what?" I asked uneasily.

"I don't know. Tell Mom?"

"What's *she* supposed to do?"

"Just watch," Grace said. Then she marched out of her bedroom.

About two minutes later, the music stopped. I could hear the sound of a screen door slamming, over and over, so I looked out. All the guests were scurrying inside like it had started thundering, and Mom was standing on the deck giving a big speech to Samantha. All I could hear was every fifth word: *intolerable, timing, Francesca, delighted.* How did those words possibly make up a sentence? I was too tired and jittery to figure it out.

The next morning at breakfast Mom informed me that I was walking Francesca to school.

"But I can't," I said through a mouthful of English muffin. "I've got plans with Nisha and Lily. We *always* walk together the first day. For good luck." Ever since fourth grade we had a set routine: I'd walk over to Nisha's and then the two of us would pick up Lily. At school we'd hang out on the grass and play Spot the Differences From Last Spring, noticing things like who had a new haircut, and whose body had gotten weirder. I wouldn't call it fun, exactly, but it helped me make it to Morning Homeroom.

"Oh, Evie, don't be so babyish," Mom said. She was unloading the dishwasher in order: knives, spoons, forks, dinner plates, salad plates, whatever plates. "Why can't you just let Francesca tag along—"

"Because we're not playing tag, Mom!"

"Hey," said Dad in a warning voice. "Don't talk to your mother that way." His BlackBerry made a windchime noise, so he took it out of his bathrobe pocket.

"I'm sorry, Dad," I said loudly. "But this is just incredibly *unfair.*"

Mom pursed her lips. "All right, Evie. It's a very busy morning and we don't have time for all this cliquish girl nonsense. Just be nice and think of Francesca's feelings. It's her first day at a new school."

"Fine. But I really wish you'd asked me first."

"*Evie,*" Dad said. Then he typed something.

The front doorbell rang.

I got up to answer it. *I am not a cliquish girl,* I told myself. I just really, really needed to walk with my two best friends on a morning when my underarms were already clammy from nerves. And why did that give Mom the right to call me names like *babyish,* just because I didn't do exactly what she wanted? I mean, she didn't even ask for my input; she just organized me like I was a piece of silverware.

And of course Dad took her side. He always did. About everything.

Gah. The first day of seventh grade was hard enough. So why did my own parents have to make it even harder?

"Oh, good morning," Francesca said, looking startled, as if I'd just showed up on *her* doorstep.

"Hi," I said. "You look nice." She was wearing a Bazooka-colored peasant top and a short yellow skirt with, like, a million flounces. And she had on those stilettos, which made her bare legs look shaky and skinny, kind of like a newborn giraffe's. But the funny thing was, she really did look nice. In a parallel-universe sort of way.

Francesca gave me the short version of her dazzling smile. "Well, thanks, Evie. So do you. Are you ready?"

I shrugged. Then I remembered something. Nisha was waiting for me at her house; I couldn't just not show up. "I have to make a quick call first, okay?" I mumbled.

Not waiting for Francesca to answer, I went back inside and speed-dialed Nisha. "Listen, I'll meet you and Lily at school, I can't explain, my Mom arranged it," I said.

"Evie?" Nisha said.

"Wait for me in front of the building." I grabbed my backpack. "BYE," I called down the hall to the kitchen, because I didn't want to leave the house in the middle of a fight. Then I double-checked to make sure I had everything: pencils, blue pens, lip gloss, keys, cell, pack of sugar-free Bubblelicious. That was when it occurred to me that Francesca wasn't carrying a backpack. In fact, she wasn't carrying anything, not even paper and pencils.

I unwrapped a stick of gum and started chomping.

We walked for half a block in the windy heat without saying a single word. The Scavullos' automatic lawn sprinkler was going *thwip, thwip, thwip*, shooting water all over the sidewalk, so mostly I just concentrated on not getting drenched. But Francesca didn't care. All of a sudden she took off her shoes, walked right over to the sprinkler, and let it spray her for as long as it took me to yell, "OMIGOD, FRANCESCA, WHAT ARE YOU DOING?" Then she ran back over to me, laughing. Maybe because of all those flounces and layers, her clothes hardly even looked damp, but her long, caramel-colored hair was definitely drippy.

"Whew. Wow. That was funfunfun," she said, stepping back into her shoes. "Don't be so boring, Evie—you should do it too. It'll wake you up!"

"I'm awake already," I answered, not too thrilled with

the word "boring." I watched her shake her hair like an overgrown puppy. "But I bet *you* were up incredibly late last night."

"Oh, I was! Aunt Sam gives the best parties. Although truthfully this one was sort of sad."

"Sad?"

"It was a cast party. For when a play is over." We started walking again. "Aunt Sam's an actress. You knew that, right?"

"How would I possibly—"

"That's odd. I thought you did." She stopped for a second to adjust her shoe strap; I noticed her foot didn't seem so peely anymore. "I guess I just assumed Aunt Sam mentioned it to your mom. Who, by the way, is utterly brilliant."

"No she's not," I said. "She's just . . . organized."

"She's terrifying. She should direct theater, the way she stormed over last night and ordered all those actors around. Aunt Sam was actually *trembling*. But your mom said you'd walk me to school today, so that was excaliburly sweet of her. And you, Evie. Thanks."

By the time we got to school, Nisha and Lily were sitting on the grass, listening to a bunch of people complain/

brag about their boring/amazing summers. Francesca had to give some "emergency forms" to the main office, so I showed her where to go. Then I plopped down beside Nisha.

"So you were walking with Malibu Barbie?" Nisha asked, watching Francesca clomp up the front steps of Blanton Middle.

"Mom forced me," I answered. "We had a huge fight about it at breakfast."

"Well, try to relax about it now," Lily said, patting my back.

"And she doesn't even *know* Francesca," I continued, definitely not relaxing. "I swear, if Mom had any clue what a liar she is—"

"Francesca lies?" Nisha asked. "Really? So it's not just that she steals ice cream?"

I looked at her. Nisha was the most honest person I knew. Too honest, sometimes. Now her eyes were wide and interested.

"She didn't exactly steal it," I said, sighing. "Anyway, you guys, let's forget about Francesca. What period is Espee?"

Nisha glanced at her schedule. "Sixth. But you're walking with us tomorrow morning, right?"

"Of course I am."

"Well, good. Because, Evie? That girl is definitely a little *off.*"

I can't tell you a whole lot about the rest of that morning because it was basically just one big blob of meeting teachers, getting textbooks, and filling out Learning Style questionnaires that were probably thrown away the second we walked out of the classroom. Most of the Hard Team teachers seemed human (or at least humanoid) and, anyway, at least they didn't make us do any actual work. The only really interesting one was the new Art teacher, Mr. Rafferty, who Lily swore looked exactly like Orlando Bloom if he were ten years older with soul patch and a really bad haircut, but Nisha said she was hallucinating.

I didn't see Francesca very much because they had her doing all sorts of Welcome to Blanton Middle–type activities. But finally, it was sixth period, which meant, drumroll, Espee's U.S. History. And I don't know how this could have happened, but somehow, instead of taking seats the way we always did—LilyEvieNisha—we ended up LilyNishaEvie. So the *very second* I sat down, Francesca slipped into the empty seat to my right. She dumped some loose papers on the desk, gave me her dazzling smile, then pointed at some writing on the whiteboard.

"SPUSH?" she practically shouted. "What's Spush, Evie?"

"It's not Spush, it's SP's U.S. History," I said. "Stephanie Pierce."

"Oh, right. Her. I met her at the New Students Breakfast. She's sort of funny, actually. They put out all these yummy pastries, but all *she* had was gallons of black coffee."

Immediately I saw the entire scene: Francesca taking random bites of fifteen different muffins, while Stephanie Pierce stood behind her, caffeinating herself for the entire school year and thinking, *What is this girl's PROBLEM?*

The classroom door opened. "See you later," Espee called to someone down the hall, then speed-walked into the classroom.

That was when Nisha started humming the Miss Gulch, Wicked Witch of the West music from *The Wizard of Oz.*

"Shut up," I hissed. "She'll hear you!"

"Evie?" Nisha said. "You okay?"

I nodded. But I didn't look at her. Instead, I was staring at Espee.

Because I'd seen her a bunch of times rushing past in

the hallw1ays. But this was the first time I'd ever seen her
up close, and after a summer of Lily's fashion magazines, I
couldn't decide if this was the weirdest-looking woman I'd
ever seen in my life, or the coolest. Aside from the tallness
and the skinniness and the random silvery streaks in her
almost-black hair, she had pale, un-made-up skin, and light
aquamarine eyes. She might have been wearing a sort of
intellectual black eyeliner, but she moved around so much,
I couldn't get a good look. And her clothes—it was hard
to imagine someone waking up for the first day of school
and thinking, *Oh, I know. I'll wear my shapeless black pants
outfit today.* But you knew she'd been thinking something,
because everything about her seemed sharp and focused
and on purpose. Even the way she grabbed a blue marker
and wrote under the word "SPUSH," in a very straight,
un-penmanshippy script:

Hïstory ïs a story we tell ourselves.

"What do you suppose this means?" she asked suddenly,
as if she'd just discovered some kind of important clue.
No one answered.
Someone in the back of the room coughed.

"It means history is a lie," called out this boy named Brendan Meyers who all of last year never once wore deodorant.

"Really?" Espee cocked her head to one side, which made her hair swing excitedly. "Then why study it?"

"Because we have to?" Kayla asked. I didn't look, but from the car alarm sound, I could tell Gaby was giggling.

"Okay, true, but that's the brainless answer," Espee said, her eyes sparkling. "What if we *didn't* have to? Would we somehow *want* to tell ourselves lies?"

"Oh, absolutely," Francesca blurted out.

"Really? Why do you say that, Francesca?"

So Espee knew her name; not a good sign. On the other hand, she was smiling. You could see she had slightly crooked teeth, which for some reason made her seem younger.

And Francesca was smiling back. "Because lies make people feel good. And maybe nobody knows the whole truth, anyway."

Omigod, I wrote in teeny-tiny letters on the first page of my Spush notebook. Francesca is sitting here admitting she's a liar!!!

"Hmm," Espee said. "Interesting. But don't we have an obligation to figure out the truth?"

"Not if lies make more sense," Francesca answered cheerfully.

She did it again!!!

"That's just stupid," Brendan snorted.

"I agree," Nisha said. "Who cares if a lie makes sense. It's just wrong."

Espee bowed her head. "Fair enough. But let's avoid words like 'stupid' and 'wrong.'"

"Even if you totally disagree with someone?" Nisha argued. She glanced quickly at Lily, who glanced quickly at me.

"Listen, guys, this is really important," Espee said firmly. "In this class, there's never just one answer, like in math. There are only *interpretations*, supported by *evidence*. So what about yours?"

I realized she was pressing on my shoulder with a cool, dry hand.

"Mine?" I said.

"Yes, you. Our note taker."

"Her name is Evie," Francesca announced. "Evie Webber." Nisha kicked me.

"Thanks, Francesca," Espee said. She looked at me as if she was expecting something important.

And then I panicked, because I'd totally lost track of this discussion. I stared blindly at the quote on the whiteboard: *History is a story we tell ourselves.* "Um. Well. I think lies always get found out, even if they *look* like they make sense. I mean, at first. But maybe . . ."

"Yes?"

"I don't think that's what the quote means. It's about stories. And stories are different from lies."

"How so?" Espee asked, speed-walking away from me. "Are stories true?"

"They don't have to be. But they could be *based* on the truth. They make more sense if they are. In the long run. And, anyway, no one *means* them to be false, so it's like they're bigger than lies."

Kayla made a face. "I have no idea what you're talking about, Evie."

"Neither do I," I admitted. A couple of kids behind me laughed.

But then I said, "Maybe stories just have more sides to them. So they're more complicated than lies. And also more interesting."

"Hmm. Very thoughtful, Evie," Espee said. Her eyes sparkled at me from across the room, and I realized I was blushing. "Well, we'll have to keep thinking about the difference between stories and lies, and why we tell ourselves U.S. history in the first place."

She reached her strong-skinny arm into a leather briefcase and took out some papers. Then she sat on top of her desk and crossed her legs like she was doing yoga.

"All right, then," she said, in a campfire sort of voice. "If history is a story, whatever that means, this year let's agree to tell ourselves the best, most fascinating story we can. So we'll be doing very little textbook work. That's the good news."

"What's the bad?" asked Brendan.

Espee smiled. She started passing around the papers.

Nisha looked at me and murmured, "Omigod, Evic. She's giving work *already*?"

I didn't answer. I just took a paper and read.

SP USH ATTIC PROJECT

Step 1: Go up to your attic. (Interpret "attic" loosely.)
Step 2: Find some family document(s) relating to a particular event or period in U.S. history—e.g., a scrapbook, a diary, some correspondence. Almost anything goes, as long as it's written.

Step 3: Analyze closely, using multiple outside sources. (Take lots of notes. Try to fill a whole spiral notebook!)

Step 4: Find out all you can about the author. What sort of storyteller is/was he/she?

—Don't have an "attic"? See me for a Mystery Box.

—Work in pairs; either person's "attic" is fine.

—Start now. Make daily progress. Finish by September 18.

chapter 4

"*Twelve days?*" Nisha screeched as we left the building. "She's giving us twelve puny days for a major research project? That she assigns to us the first day of school? I swear, you guys, that woman definitely *is* a wicked witch."

"Actually," Lily said, "I feel kind of sorry for her."

Nisha laughed in disbelief. "You do? Why?"

"Because she obviously has no life."

"How can you tell that?" I asked curiously.

"Just the way she's so intense about everything. Like she really thinks U.S. history is so important. And interesting. And also the way she looks."

"Omigod. Her hair. Those *pants*," Nisha hooted. "Almost goth. *Nerd* goth."

"There's no such thing as nerd goth," I said. "Besides, I think she looks sort of cool."

"Right. And you also like bug jewelry."

I pretended to ignore that. "Anyway, who cares what she *looks* like? Don't you think she's incredibly un-teachery? I mean, compared to, like, Mr. Womack?" Last year Mr. Womack was our teacher for sixth-grade Social Studies. All he did the whole year were these dorky PowerPoint presentations with the same title: *The Legacy of Ancient Greece, The Legacy of Ancient Rome, The Legacy of Fill in the Blank.*

"I still think she's evil, assigning this huge project the very first day," Nisha grumbled. "And then acting like there's no right or wrong, even if someone is lying."

Before I could say that I actually didn't think that's what Espee had meant, Lily grabbed my arm. "Look, Evie, is that Zane?" With her non-grabbing hand, she pointed to a clump of jersey-wearing eighth-grade boys on the grass in front of the faculty parking lot.

"Uh, yeah, it is," I said. I squinted as if he were a tiny, smudgy dot way off in the distance. "I mean, I'm pretty sure."

Lily grinned. "So why don't you go over and talk to him, then?"

"And say what? 'One scoop of chocolate chip, please'?"

"No. You could say something like, 'Hey, Zane. I heard you had Espee last year. Is she actually a wicked witch, or does she just dress like one?'"

I groaned. I mean, I loved Lily, but she kind of thought she was an expert on flirting and dating just because she went to the mall last June with Tyler Corbett. And really, it was barely even a date. Tyler's mom left them at a booth at the IHOP and then went off to shop at Payless, and the only thing Tyler said to Lily *the entire time* was, *Can you please pass the syrup?* So that's what we've called him ever since: Can You Please Pass the Syrup. Of course not to his face.

"Oh, leave her alone, Lily," Nisha said. "Evie doesn't even like Zane, remember?"

"That's not what I said," I protested. "I said I wasn't sure."

Nisha grinned at me. "Well, that's not my *interpretation*. Based on the *evidence*."

Pretty soon we were at Nisha's. We'd be going there all the time now, because Mrs. Guptil had convinced Lily's dad to let Lily do homework there in the afternoons rather than be totally unsupervised in a messy house full of junk food. I was happy for Lily, who I knew sometimes got lonely with no one home all day except Jimmy. But to be honest, I wasn't so sure about this new arrangement, mainly because we'd have to be dealing with Nisha's mom on a daily basis.

"And how was school?" Mrs. Guptil asked, pouncing on us the second we walked in the door. "Did you like all your teachers?"

Nisha opened the refrigerator. "Meh."

"What does 'meh' mean? Speak English, Nisha, my darling."

"They seem okay," Lily told Mrs. Guptil. Then she turned bright pink. "Especially the art teacher."

"Oh, yeah, Mr. Rafferty's definitely hot," Nisha said. "But I'm not so sure about that little soul-patch thingy. It's kind of 'I'm so cool, I'm not really a grown-up.' Don't you think, Evie?"

Mrs. Guptil made a *tsk* sound. "Nisha, my darling, show some respect for your teacher, please. And shut the refrigerator if you're not taking anything out."

Nisha grabbed a bunch of green grapes. She popped a couple in her mouth, then offered the rest to Lily and me. "So, Moms," she said ultra-casually, in a way I knew Mrs. Guptil hated, "do we still have Great-grandpa's scrapbook?"

"Of course we do," Mrs. Guptil said. "It's in the attic. Do you think I'd just creep up there one day and toss it in the garbage? It's your *heritage*, Nisha, my darling." She shook her head at Lily and me. "My daughter is such an American," she said, sighing.

After we finished the grapes and listened to Mrs. Guptil complain about her landscaper, Nisha went up to her attic and came back down to her bedroom with a big leather box. As soon as she opened it, I knew it was incredible. I mean, totally apart from the fact that it was like the whole Attic Project was lying there on her bed, all ready for Step 3, it was just an amazing thing to see: an enormous scrapbook covered in purple silk, with thick cardboardy pages full of faded photos and typed letters and fountain-pen-written notes. All of it was about Nisha's great-grandpa Mohan, who'd been a doctor back in Delhi. He was great at it, Nisha said, but when he came to Baltimore in the twenties, no hospital would hire him because his skin was dark and he had an accent. So he worked as a janitor in the local veterans hospital, and became president of the Baltimore Socialist Party. He sent a million letters and photos back to India, which some relative stuck in a scrapbook. And one day when he was visiting Delhi, the relative gave him the scrapbook to bring home to Baltimore.

"And now it's mine," Nisha said, making a cartoon mustache with her index finger. "All mine."

"Plus whoever you're working with," I said. Then I bit my lower lip. "So how are we going to decide who's working with who?"

"Maybe we don't have to," Lily said in a soothing voice. "Maybe Espee will let us all work together."

"She won't," I insisted. "The assignment is to work in pairs. Meaning one attic, two people. Not three."

Lily put her arm around my shoulders. "Let's talk to her tomorrow, okay? We'll explain how we are."

I nodded. "What if she says no?"

"Then we'll deal with it," Nisha said confidently. "Besides, what are you so worried about? After that answer you gave today, you're totally her pet."

"I'm not—"

"Yes you are. You and Francesca. Who's all in favor of lying."

Later, when I got home, Grace was sitting in the kitchen doing her AP Calculus. She immediately told me Francesca had called. Twice. And wanted me to call her back.

"Okay, thanks," I said, not reaching for the phone.

Because I had a pretty good idea what the call was about:
She wanted to pair up on the Attic Project.

Grace carefully erased something in her notebook. "So
how was your first day?"

"I survived." I opened the fridge, even though I wasn't
hungry. "When you had Espee you had that Attic Project,
right?"

"Oh, who remembers *seventh grade*?" She gave me one of
her superior smiles. "Oh, riiiight. You mean where we had to
find family junk in the attic and then do all this research?"

I nodded. "And was there anything?"

"Of *course* not. You think Mom would keep any of that
stuff? The way she cleans?"

I closed the fridge and got a gigantic glass of ice cubes
out of the freezer. "So did you look anywhere else? I mean,
besides the attic."

"Well, sure," Grace said. "I called every single one of our
relatives, and I spent the entire Labor Day weekend going
through Grandma Nora's file cabinet. And you know what
I discovered? We're probably the only history-free family in
North America."

I chomped on a cube. "So what did you do? The Mystery
Box?"

"Yeah. And it wasn't even a box. It was just a stack of letters from a soldier in World War Two. Which I was positive Espee wrote herself."

"How could you tell?"

"I don't know. They were handwritten, but the ink seemed too perfect, and he mentioned too many battles. And of course we had to analyze every little picky detail, so it was a ton of extra work." She blinked at me. "Why? You're doing a Box?"

"I might have to. If I can't work with Nisha."

"Well, make sure you work with Nisha, then. Because the Box was really evil. At least in my personal experience."

The phone rang. I checked the caller ID: S PATTISON. Again.

"Don't answer that, okay?" I begged. "I'm sort of hiding from Francesca."

"That's ridiculous," Grace said. "She's right next door. What if she was watching through the window? What if she saw you come home just now?"

"It's really not my problem, Grace."

She superior-smiled at that and reopened her AP Calculus book. Which meant the conversation was over because Grace Had to Study, even though the kitchen phone kept right on ringing and ringing.

chapter 5

N o," said Ms. Pierce when we went to her classroom at lunch the next day.

"But we're so *good* together," Lily said. "We never fight."

"And we always share the work," I added. "And we respect each other's opinions." That was totally overdoing it, of course, but I was starting to really freak.

"Sorry," Espee said, shaking her strange hair. "I've been doing this project for eleven years now, girls, and I've learned the hard way that groups of three just never work out. Someone is always left in the cold."

"Not us," Nisha insisted. "You can ask Mr. Womack."

I nodded at her. That was a smart thing to say.

But Espee wasn't buying it. "Sorry," she repeated firmly. "I truly am, but I'm afraid this one isn't negotiable. Just figure out how you want to partner up, and then let me know by sixth period."

"But that's impossible," I wailed.

Espee pressed a cool, dry hand on my shoulder, the way she did the day before in class. "Come talk to me if it really is," she said.

As soon as we were out in the hall, Nisha exploded. "She's so nasty! And condescending! The way she judged our friendship. Like she even knows anything *about* us."

"Oh, well," Lily said, sighing. "We'll figure something out."

We went to the cafeteria, but by that time all the lines were a million miles long, and anyway, I wasn't super-hungry. Nisha and Lily were, though, so they got on the Wraps line while I saved a table and nervous-nibbled a bag of Sun Chips. Across the room I watched Francesca eating a slice of pizza by herself, which sort of gave me a guilty pang. The next table over, Zane was shoving around those jersey-wearing boys from yesterday, and for about two horrible seconds I thought she was going to go over to him and ask for lunch recommendations. But she didn't. She just finished her slice and left the cafeteria, and I could tell one of the jersey-wearers even made some kind of gross Neanderthalish comment as she clomped past.

Then from out of nowhere Kayla showed up at Zane's table and started flirting and laughing, like they were suddenly such great friends. That was really weird, because everyone in the seventh grade knew that Kayla was sort-of-dating this semi-jock eighth grader named Ryan Esposito. Plus, when I ran into her and Gaby at I Scream the other day, she didn't even talk to Zane. Of course, she was behind me in line; so maybe they had a whole flirty conversation while I was outside with Francesca, gaping at her empty pockets.

"Well, so here's the problem," Nisha announced as she and Lily sat down with their wraps. "You know I'd love to partner with you, Evie, and obviously so would Lily. But since Lily is doing homework at my house every afternoon, the only thing that makes sense for this stupid project is if she pairs up with me."

I looked at Lily. She was turning hot pink and poking lettuce back into her wrap.

"Right," I said slowly. "I totally forgot about the whole after-school thing."

"Then you're not mad?" Nisha asked, watching me with worried eyes.

"Of course not. Lily's at your house, anyway. So yeah, it makes perfect sense."

"We'll switch for the next assignment, okay?"

"Sure," I said. But I was thinking: *Lily will still be at your house for the next assignment. And probably for all the assignments the entire rest of the year. So how will it ever "make sense" to partner up with me?*

Now Lily was patting my arm. "Thanks for being so great about this, Evie. So who do you think you'll work with?"

I swallowed. "I don't know."

"Ask Brendan Meyers," Nisha said.

I made a face.

"What's wrong with him? He's using deodorant now; he's fine."

"Well, maybe he doesn't *smell*, Nisha, but he has all this extra *spit*. And every time he talks—"

"Okay, whatever. We're trying to eat here. How about Katie Finberg?"

"She's very nice." I sighed.

"But?"

"But I don't know. Don't you think she's a little too perfect-perfect?"

Out of the corner of my eye I could see Gaby sit down with Kayla and Zane.

Lily shrugged. "Maybe. But don't you *want* someone who works incredibly hard?"

"Yeah, I guess," I said, crumpling my Sun Chips bag to drown out Gaby's horrible laugh. "And she might be the best person left. Anyway, I'll think about it, you guys."

"Great," Nisha replied, smiling at us both like everything was all decided.

In the hallway outside her classroom, Espee was talking to Mr. Rafferty. As soon as he saw me he said something in her ear, then walked away, grinning.

She swung her hair at me. "What's up, Evie?" she asked in a friendly voice.

So I told her what had happened, how I needed a partner. "I was thinking maybe Katie Finberg," I added. "If she's free."

"Unfortunately, I believe Katie's working with Brendan

Meyers. And you know, most of the pairs are set by now."
She smiled, her pale aquamarine eyes lighting up. "What
about Francesca Pattison?"

"You mean as a partner?"

"Well, she's looking for one, and just this morning
she asked me about you. Why? Is there a problem with
Francesca?"

I shook my head. No problems at all, unless you counted
the fact that the girl was a total liar. And wore weird cos-
tumes. And ran in front of sprinklers. "Isn't there anybody
else?" I asked hopefully.

"Not that I know of," Espee replied, with a little frown
in her voice. "This is seventh grade, Evie; I'm not going to
figure this out for you. You're welcome to ask around, but I'll
need to know by the end of today."

Then she turned around and speed-walked into the
classroom. If she had come right out and called me *babyish*,
the way Mom had yesterday at breakfast, it wouldn't have
felt any worse.

"Hi, Evie, did you get my phone messages yesterday?"
Francesca asked the second I sat down.

"Yes. Sorry. I've just been really busy," I said, opening
my Spush notebook.

"Me too. But I was calling about the Attic Project. I have this *staggering* old diary. From the San Francisco Earthquake!"

Nisha kicked me.

"You do?" I said, kicking her back.

"From my great-great-aunt Angelica Beaumont. She was sixteen when it happened, utterly gorgeous and fabulously rich, and absolutely *everybody* was in love with her."

"Kind of like Paris Hilton?" Nisha asked innocently.

Francesca laughed. "Oh no, not at all. She was an artist. And an intellectual. And I believe a suffragette."

"A what?" Lily said, leaning over.

"Woman who fought for the right to vote," I told her.

"Cool," Lily said, glancing at Nisha.

Francesca nodded proudly. "She was all alone in her mansion when the earthquake hit. Almost everything she owned was completely destroyed, but she never stopped writing in her diary. Even with all the chandeliers swaying."

"Awesome," said Nisha, trying not to laugh. "I mean, truthfully, Francesca, it almost sounds unbelievable."

"I know," Francesca said. "I'm blessed just to have it."

Nisha rolled her eyes at me.

barbara dee

Right at that moment Espee started talking, and so class officially started. And I know this sounds exactly like that scene in every horror movie, where the heroine is about to walk into the haunted house, and you're yelling at the screen, *JUST DON'T. JUST WALK AWAY, YOU IDIOT, BEFORE IT'S TOO LATE.* And I swear, I completely understood that the sane thing to do at that point would have been to say, *So sorry, Francesca. I've already made plans, have fun with your diary,* and leave it at that.

But I thought about walking around the Spush classroom, begging unclaimed people to "partner up" on a Mystery Box. I thought about Nisha telling me who I was supposed to work with, and then making fun of Francesca for wanting to. I thought about Francesca eating lunch by herself, and how horrible I'd been for avoiding her, not even returning her phone calls, slipping out of the house superearly this morning so I could walk to school in private with Nisha and Lily.

Oh, and I thought about something else, too: the way she'd called me *boring* yesterday because I wouldn't go in the sprinkler. She was right; I was boring. My entire life was boring. And whatever else it was, this was a chance to make it unboring.

So I waited for Espee to be writing some long philosophical quote on the whiteboard. Then I leaned over to Francesca and whispered, "That diary sounds great. Of course I'll work with you."

She gave me her dazzling smile. "Oh, I knew you would," she said.

chapter 6

Y ou're WHAT?" Nisha shrieked. We were at the lockers, where, like, the entire seventh grade was hanging out before dismissal.

"Katie Finberg was taken," I whispered. "And Francesca needed a partner."

"So why is that *your* problem?"

"It's not. But she has that diary—"

"*If* she has that diary. Evie, I don't know how to tell you this, but you're making a huge mistake."

"How do you know that?" I asked, pretending to fight with my jacket zipper.

"Oh, come on, Evie," Lily murmured. "You said you

didn't trust her. Isn't there anybody else?"

"Not really. Espee said—"

"Hey, Evie, are you ready to go?" Suddenly Francesca was standing at my locker. She was wearing a rainbow-tie-dyed poncho, a purple miniskirt, and black tights with little silver stars on them. Oh yes, and cowboy boots. It was maybe the weirdest outfit I'd seen her in so far, and my eyes couldn't figure out where to focus.

"Um, Evie?" Nisha was saying in a strangely loud voice. "Did you forget what you just told me?"

"What?"

"*You know,*" she said, her eyes shooting message-beams. "That doctor appointment thingy. That you just remembered was this afternoon."

I stared back at her. "Oh, yeah," I muttered. "The doctor appointment. Actually, Nisha, I rescheduled that."

"Are you *sure* you should have?"

"Uh-huh. Definitely."

"Because you were feeling so sick before. *Weren't* you?"

Okay, this was going way too far. Nisha was only trying to rescue me, obviously, and I knew I should have been grateful. But was she going to stand here and insist that I dump Francesca in front of everyone? And also act like I couldn't make a decision for myself? "Well, I'm fine *now*," I said firmly. "So stop worrying about me."

And then, with probably the whole school gawking at us, plus Nisha and Lily whispering and frowning, I left the building with Francesca Pattison.

As soon as we were outside, I wanted to get down to business, ask about the "staggering old diary" and also about her great-great-aunt's incredibly unboring life. But before I could even open my mouth, Francesca said something that almost made me choke on my Bubblelicious: "Okay, Evie, so tell me *all* about Zane."

"Excuse me?"

"Zane. Your boyfriend?"

"He's not my boyfriend." I spat my blobby gum into a tissue, then stuffed the tissue into my jeans pocket.

"But I told you, I'm psychic about these things." Francesca was smiling. "And I can tell you're madly in love with him."

"I'm not—"

"Okay, let me put it this way: You have a massive passionate *crush*. But you don't have the slightest idea what to do about it. Am I getting warmer?"

I felt my cheeks burning. "Okay. Um, no offense, Francesca, but it's kind of none of your business. Can we please just talk about Angelica Beaumont?"

"Of course! If Zane is a painful subject, let's *absolutely* talk about Angelica." She did the heart attack thing. "Don't you adore her name, Evie? Although I wonder what her friends called her. Maybe Angie. Or Angel."

"You don't know?"

"How would I?"

"You have the diary, right?"

"In my hands? Oh, *no*, Evie, my great-grandmother does."

"Who?"

"Angelica's baby sister Isabel. In San Francisco."

I blinked. "Well, so how are we going to get it, then?"

"We'll write to her. This afternoon."

"Shouldn't we call? Wouldn't that be faster?"

"Well, yes, but Isabel doesn't hear well on the phone. Believe me, I've tried, and so has Aunt Sam. It's utterly hopeless."

"What about e-mail?"

"She's ninety-four years old, Evie. I sincerely doubt she e-mails."

A few minutes later we were standing in front of our two houses. A teeny frantic voice in my head was whispering: *JUST GO HOME, EVIE. IT'S NOT TOO LATE FOR A MYSTERY BOX, EVEN IF YOU HAVE TO WORK ALL BY YOURSELF.* But I told the voice to shut up; I was going to do this thing with Francesca. Starting now.

"We could write the letter at my house," I offered, not very enthusiastically. "As long as we're super-quiet. Grace has an SAT tutor this afternoon."

"On the second day of school?" Francesca said. "Help, how alarming. Let's just go to Aunt Sam's."

"Is she home?"

"Yes, I think so. Wait, hold it, she's in the city this afternoon, auditioning for a soap. Reading for the part of the vixen scientist. Isn't that hilarious?" She turned her key in the door. "Topaz? Tourmaline? Hey, little girls, I'm home."

I expected two miniature poodles with pedicures and poofy haircuts to come yapping over to greet her, but the house stayed dark and quiet. So then Francesca pulled off her poncho, kicked off her cowboy boots, and turned on every light in the entry. Way down the front hall I spotted something lumpish and gray, like a dusty old bedroom slipper. Suddenly it hopped away.

"Topaz!" Francesca cried. "Have you been chewing up the rugs again?"

"Was that a *rabbit*?" I practically shrieked.

She nodded, laughing. "Aunt Sam's true loves. Other than gorgeous Tristan, but alas, he broke her heart."

"Wait. Wait. Her heart was broken by a *rabbit*?"

"What? No, Evie, don't be an imbecile. Tristan Royce is an *actor*. Was. In the play that just ended." Francesca walked into the living room, which had huge, cream-colored pillows, and CDs, all over the floor, and the heavy leftover wine-and-perfume smell of Samantha's party. One corner of the coffee-colored rug was in shreds; Francesca got on her knees and tied the wool strands into little knots, then tucked them underneath.

"So, anyway," she continued calmly, as if covering up for rabbit vandalism was something she did all the time, "now they're both looking for new acting jobs. And new relationships, too. It's all so deeply tragic, don't you think? Oh well, c'est la vie. Are you hungry?"

"Starving." All I'd had for lunch was Sun Chips, and I'd

barely eaten those. I followed Francesca into the stainless-steel kitchen, which looked shiny and empty, as if it had been used maybe a total of three times. She opened the enormous fridge.

"Take what you want," she said, waving her hand. "We're absolutely loaded from the party. None of those actors ever eat anything, so we'll be living off this junk *forever.*"

I looked inside. Someone—was it Samantha?—had crammed in all the leftovers without wrapping anything, so it was like this one big cheese puff/sushi/guacamole/salsa/shish-kebob stew. Plus in the way back of the fridge there were huge Glad bags of lettuce leaves, which I guessed was what Topaz and Tourmaline ate when they weren't gorging on wool.

"Uh, thanks. Maybe later," I said.

Francesca looked disappointed. Then suddenly her eyes widened. "I know," she said.

She opened the freezer and pulled out five quarts of I Scream—Triple Fudge Marshmallow Chunk, Golden Brownie with Caramel Fudge Ripple, Peanut Butter Chip Cookie Dough, plus two others with the labels peeled off—and then grabbed two spoons.

I stared in shock. "More party food?"

"Oh, no. Actors don't eat *ice cream*. Well, actually, Aunt Sam sneak-eats it late at night when she thinks I'm asleep. Here." She handed me a spoon. "So does Grace sneak-eat?"

"Grace? Of course not. She's way too self-disciplined."

"Oh, I bet she does, Evie. To work off all that academic stress. What about your mom?"

I laughed. "*Never.*"

She pulled off all five lids and licked the insides. "Veggie burgers and salad every night for dinner, right? God, you must be so sick of it."

"Well, sometimes," I admitted. "But of course it's good for you. I mean, you're supposed to eat that way, right?"

"I guess." She screwed up her face. "But I really just detest all those bloody *rules*."

I dipped my spoon into the Triple Fudge Marshmallow Chunk: just the perfect temperature, slightly melty, but not soup. "Was that why you left your old school?" I asked casually.

"Because of the food? Don't be silly." She took a gigantic spoonful of Unlabeled. Then she grinned at me. "Evie," she said. "Here's a burning question: Do you think Espee sneak-eats?"

I laughed so hard, a gob of marshmallow went up my nose. *"What?"*

"Because I'm positive she does. Here's my theory: I think she's desperately lonely, but she throws herself into her work. And then late at night when she simply can't bear to confront her romantic yearnings, she eats a pint of—what is this? Dark Chocolate Snickers Truffle."

"Are you psychotic? Where did you get that from?"

"I'm psychic. Not *psychotic*, Evie. Slight difference." She stuck her spoon in the Triple Fudge Marshmallow Chunk. "Don't you wonder about her? I do. Because she's obviously a deep person. So I can't imagine all she cares about is teaching boring U.S. History to boring seventh graders. Especially in Blanton."

"Hey, Blanton's not so bad," I protested.

She ignored that. "You've seen those posters on her walls. She's traveled all over the world. So why is she wasting her life *here*? Unless," she added dramatically, "she has some dark, romantic secret."

"Like what?"

She leaned forward, breathing chocolate in my face. "I'll tell you, but you can't tell anyone else."

I nodded.

"I'm convinced," she practically whispered, "that she's passionately in love with Mr. Rafferty."

"WHAT?"

"Yesterday I saw them chatting in the main office. And I saw them right before dismissal today, in the hall outside her classroom. She was gazing into his eyes as if her soul was on fire. Or don't you believe me?"

"I believe you," I said, laughing. "I just think you're crazy."

"Why?" She raised one eyebrow. "Just because she's cool and deep and intellectual, you think she's incapable of crushing on the one truly gorgeous male in the entire school?"

"That's not what I meant! And frankly, I don't even want to be thinking about this!"

She pointed her spoon at me. "Okay. I've figured out your problem, Evie. You're terrified of your own romantic imagination." Then she tossed the spoon into the sink. "And that's why you're so paralyzed about Zane."

"Excuse me?"

"I'll shut up now. See? Lipstotallysealed. Can'teventalk. Omigod." She jumped up. "I forgot about the vitamins."

She ran out of the kitchen without even putting the ice

cream back in the freezer. I had no idea what was going on, but I guessed that, since she got rid of her spoon, she was done eating. So I put the lids back on the pints and lined them up on the middle freezer shelf. Then I walked out into the living room.

Which was empty.

chapter 7

U h, Francesca?" I called. "Hello?"

No answer. From somewhere I could hear the air conditioner rumble on, like a huge lion snoring. It made the house seem bigger. And emptier.

"FRANCESCA?" I called again.

"Shhhh," she answered from over my head.

I looked up. She was standing on the second-floor landing holding a tiny bottle of something. "Come upstairs," she whispered. *"Qui-et-ly."*

I kicked off my sandals and climbed the stairs. Just as I got to the top, she suddenly lunged. "GOT YOU," she shouted, grabbing a white puffy bedroom slipper.

Only it wasn't—it was a rabbit. The other one. Tourmaline.

She squirted something from a little dropper into the rabbit's mouth. Then she opened her arms and it hopped frantically down the hallway.

"One down," she said, grinning at me. "Now for Topaz. Oh, Tooo-paaaz," she sang in an Elmer Fudd sort of voice. "Come and get your din-din."

Laughing our heads off, we tiptoed from room to room, searching for the dustball-colored, rug-chewing little beast. I realized that while I was wabbit-hunting, I was also getting an up-close tour of Samantha Pattison's house, and it shocked me how normal it was: just a bunch of sand-colored guest bedrooms no one seemed to be actually using. It occurred to me that one of those rooms belonged to Francesca, but really, they were all so blank, you couldn't even tell which one.

Finally Francesca sighed. "She's probably in Aunt Sam's boudoir. Which is strictly off limits to rodents, but Topaz is kind of a free spirit. Are your feet clean?"

"My *feet*?"

"Sorry to ask, but Aunt Sam's a bit compulsive about her

room." She opened the door very slowly, and we tiptoed in.

And I gasped. I mean, literally *gasped.*

Because it was the most amazing room I'd ever seen, like a contest in one of Lily's magazines: "Enter Our Sweepstakes and Win the Bedroom of Your Dreams!"

Samantha Pattison had a gigantic canopy bed. With an actual canopy. Not some dorky Hello Kitty canopy, either—this one was deep purple and gauzy, with matching deep purple sheets and, like, a million rose silk pillows. She had a cream-colored vanity with a chair—a throne, really—covered in that same gorgeous rose color, and a curvy-legged writing desk facing rose-curtained windows. And hanging from the ceiling was an enormous crystal chandelier, which was going *plinka plinka plinka* from a light perfumy breeze.

"Oh. My. God," I said, stepping carefully on the velvety cream-colored carpeting. "Whoa, Francesca."

"Staggering, huh?" She yanked me inside. "Look at this."

She led me through Samantha's private bathroom, which had floor-to-ceiling mirrors and a circular whirlpool bath and perfectly folded rose-colored towels all mono-grammed <SP>. And then before I realized we'd even left the bathroom, we were in another room—which wasn't even a room.

It was a closet. I swear: a giant room-size *closet*. With racks and racks of clothes—dresses, gowns, nightgowns, you name it, some of them in colors I'd never seen except in Lily's magazines. Also fabrics: satin, velvet, lamé. Against one wall was a tower—sort of a bookcase, actually—full of shoes. (A lot of them were super-fancy, so it was obvious where Francesca got her stilettos.) Stacked up against the other wall were, like, twenty huge wicker baskets with hand-written labels: GLOVES. WRAPS. CLUTCHES. SARONGS. *Sarongs?* I tried to remember if I'd come across any *sarongs* in Lily's magazines, but I was too gaga to even think straight.

"Why does she have so much stuff?" I managed to ask.

"Oh, you know," said Francesca vaguely. She lifted a coppery gown from the rack and held it against herself. But it only came up to her shins, and didn't make it all the way across her waist. "She's been in lots of plays. And soaps, of course. And she knows a lot of costume people, obviously."

She started dancing around in big loopy circles. "Evie, can you imagine genius Espee wearing something like *this*?"

"No, I can't," I said quickly. "Of course not."

"Me neither. Alas." She re-hung-up the dress, not noticing that one shoulder slid right off the hanger. "Wouldn't it be so epic if she did, though? Wonder what Theo Rafferty would say. Oh, wait a sec, look at this."

She pulled down a wicker basket labeled VINTAGE. Inside was one giant tangle of silver chains and stretchy bracelets and earrings.

"Oh, help," said Francesca, looking embarrassed. "What a disaster."

"What happened? It looks like a hurricane hit it."

"Probably the rabbits."

'The *rabbits*? You mean they come in here and play dress-up?"

She sighed. "Okay, it was me. I was looking for something, and I lost track. So help me fix it, okay?"

We sat on the floor untangling what we could. Francesca's nails were longer than mine, so she was better at it, and the way she was able to free the snarls by rolling the chains in her fingertips made me think she had done this before. Finally she held up a heart-shaped silver locket on an almost completely knot-free chain.

"Look at this," she said. "Gorgeous, huh?"

I took it from her. Under the chandelier light, you could see the initials SP and TR inscribed in a fancy, hard-to-read, old-fashioned script: *SP. TR.*

"Very elegant," I said. "Does your aunt ever wear it?"

"Lord no. It was a present from Tristan Royce. As far as Aunt Sam is concerned, he can absolutely fry. Ooh, wait, Evie, I think I've got them. Here," she said, forcing something into my hand.

Immediately I recognized the long, fancy earrings Francesca was wearing at Staples. The golden chandeliers. The Oscar earrings.

"You like them? Try them on. Don't worry," she added, before I could argue. "They aren't even real."

She grabbed a hand mirror that was lying around somewhere and held it up for me. I slipped off my own tiny silver hoops that I'd bought at the mall last summer, and slipped on the long, dangly gold ones.

Then I peeked at myself.

I moved my head. The earrings swished.

Plinka, plinka, plinka.

"All right, Evie, now listen to me: You're keeping them," Francesca said, laughing. "No arguments."

I took a breath. "Don't be crazy, Francesca."

"Why not? Aunt Sam has a million others; she won't even notice they're gone. Or care. And, anyway, they look utterly brilliant on you."

I had to admit they did. They shimmered. They lit up my used-to-be-blonder hair. They made my eyes glow.

But. "They belong to your aunt," I said. "Besides, I'd never wear something like this. In a majillion years."

"I know," she said thoughtfully. "And that's your problem."

I pretend-laughed. "My problem is I won't wear these earrings? I thought you said my problem was—"

"Your *problem*, Evie, is that you have all these bloody *rules* about yourself. Good earrings and bad earrings. Chocolate chip ice cream and veggie burgers. You know, sometimes your life just needs a little jolt."

"Oh, come on, Francesca. I didn't say they were *bad*—"

Suddenly we heard a door bang open. "FRANCES-CAAAA," a loud voice called.

"Help, it's Aunt Sam," Francesca muttered. "We shouldn't be in here."

She yanked my arm.

"Wait," I hissed. "The earrings."

"No time," she said. "Just take them, Evie. *Go.*"

She shoved me into the hall. I ran down the steps and slipped my feet into my sandals.

"Where are you, sugarpie?" Samantha Pattison called from the kitchen.

"Coming," Francesca answered casually.

I snatched my backpack, which I'd left at the front door when we spotted the rabbit. And it was only when I was nearly three-quarters of the way home that I realized we'd never written that letter to Angelica Beaumont's sister.

hen I walked into the kitchen, Mom was on her cell, stir-frying some veggies with her other hand. "I completely agree, the mudroom is hopeless," she was saying. "And my professional advice is, get rid of that wall. Yup. Just rent a bulldozer and knock the whole thing down." She noticed me. "Dinner in ten minutes," she mouthed.

I nodded, which made the earrings jiggle. So I immediately stopped nodding.

The kitchen phone rang.

"Just a minute, Caroline," Mom said into her cell. "Evie, can you answer it, please? Bring it into the living room, take down any messages, and then immediately go wash up for dinner."

Yes, Your Majesty, I thought. I moved an earring out of the way, and picked up the receiver. "Hello?"

"Evie? Where've you been?" Nisha was asking. She sounded worried. "Why didn't you answer your cell? I've been calling you all afternoon."

"Sorry," I said. "My cell was in my backpack. And I was at Francesca's but I kind of got distracted."

"With what?"

"Oh, you know. Talking about the project."

"Really? Well, you're excused." She rolled her eyes. I mean, over the phone I couldn't hear her eyeballs actually rolling, but I was sure that's what she was doing. That's how well I knew her. "So how did it go?" she asked.

"Fine, actually. We had the house to ourselves."

"Sweet." She paused. "And did she let you try on all her glamorous little outfits?"

"Hey, Nisha, I *like* how she dresses. It's original."

She didn't answer. Which in a way *was* an answer. Then she said, "And you read the diary? It actually exists?"

"Of course it exists."

"Well, I'm glad for you, then. At least it wasn't a total waste of time."

"Right," I said. I could hear Mom in the kitchen doing her Delightful Laugh. "No, it wasn't."

"Aaanyway," Nisha said. Her cell was making a *swooshy* noise; probably she was moving to a Mrs. Guptil–free location. Or trying to. "Have you heard about Kayla? She's going around telling everyone she likes Zane. She says he's, like, the cutest boy in the eighth grade, and that he's quote-unquote sensitive."

"To what?"

"I don't know. Her, I guess."

I bit my lip. "I thought she was going out with Ryan."

"They broke up. She caught him texting Sierra Kaufman."

"Oh. Well, that's . . . interesting."

"You don't even care?"

"Why should I? Kayla can like whoever she wants."

"Okay, Evie. I just thought you'd want to hear about it before school tomorrow." Nisha sighed. It sounded like a tornado in my ear. "So you're meeting us in the morning, right?"

"Actually," I said quickly, "can you wait a few minutes if

I'm late? I need to return something to Francesca first."

"Oh yeah? What?"

"It's kind of a long story." I suddenly felt warm, as if I'd shoplifted the earrings and just felt a security guard's tap on my shoulder.

But apparently Nisha wasn't in the mood for a long story. "I don't know," she said slowly. "Because if you're going over to Francesca's in the morning, won't she want to walk with you?"

"I guess."

"So maybe we should just meet you at school."

"You sure? I'll be really quick, I promise."

"It'll just be easier. I'll tell Lily." Then she hung up.

I went upstairs, surprised and hurt that my best friends were refusing to wait for me, even if (and we didn't know this for a fact) Francesca would be tagging along. Plus, I really didn't appreciate hearing all that stuff about Kayla and Zane. And why was Nisha obsessing about my Attic Project? It felt like she almost *wanted* the diary to be a fake. Which was incredibly weird of her, and also unfair. Because she had that amazing scrapbook; why should she even care about the diary?

So it was perfectly okay that I'd lied to her about seeing

it, I told myself. Even though technically I didn't even lie:
all I said was that the diary *existed*. And I had no reason to
think that wasn't true.

But by now it was starting to bother me that we hadn't
written that letter to Isabel Beaumont. How exactly had
we lost track of it? I tried to think about the long afternoon, how one thing had just led to another, like a rabbit
scampering around a big, empty house. I couldn't let Francesca mix me up like that, I scolded myself. Not if we were
going to be partners on this project. I had to stand up
to her, make sure we got focused. And I would. Starting
tomorrow.

I locked myself in the bathroom and stared in the
mirror. I swished the earrings. I shook my head. I nodded
like crazy. *Oh yes, Zane, I'd love to go with you to the movies
on Saturday. Yes, Fudge Caramel Whatever is MY favorite
flavor too!* The earrings still went *plinka plinka plinka*, but
in the privacy of my own bathroom they just looked wrong.
I didn't think they were *bad earrings*, I told my reflection in
the mirror. It's just that they were all Hollywood starlety,
and I was more of a mosquito-in-amber sort of person.

So I slipped them off, wrapped them up in some toilet
paper, and immediately washed my hands for dinner.

❀

At seven the next morning I rang Samantha Pattison's bell. It was one of those obnoxious Big Ben chimes that took, like, thirty seconds to shut up, and I was terrified it would wake the whole street. But finally Francesca opened the door wearing a purple satin bathrobe.

"Evie," she said, squinting in the sunlight. "You're so early."

"Sorry. I wanted to give you back these." I forced the toilet-paper wad of earrings into her hand.

She blinked at them. "Oh, you didn't have to. I told you, Aunt Sam has thousands—"

"I know," I interrupted. "They're really, really nice. But I felt funny about just taking them like that. Thanks anyway."

She shrugged. "Come in. I need to get dressed."

"Thanks, but I'll just wait here." Probably I was overdoing the Standing Up to Francesca routine, but I was thinking that if I went into Samantha's house, we'd start chasing rabbits or something, and then somehow we'd forget all about Morning Homeroom.

About five minutes later she showed up at the door wearing lime green biking shorts, black patent-leather ankle boots, and a short, white zebra-patterned jacket trimmed with black fur. Immediately I imagined another snarky comment from Nisha. "Don't worry, it's faux," she said, fluffing up her collar.

"I wasn't worried about that," I said truthfully. "But aren't you kind of boiling?"

"Maybe a tad. Oh, well. We'll just have to find another lawn sprinkler—"

"Gah. *No*, Francesca."

"Only kidding! My God. You take everything so seriously."

"Not everything," I insisted.

We started walking, and I yelled at myself, *NOW! SAY IT NOW. DON'T LET HER GET YOU DISTRACTED!* So I added, "But can I say something? I *am* really serious about our Attic Project. And I'm a little upset we never wrote that letter yesterday."

She gave me the semi-dazzling smile. "Oh, *don't* worry, Evie. I took care of it last night."

"You mean you wrote it? By yourself?"

"Uh-huh. Aunt Sam has the most brilliant stationery."

"That's great," I said, wondering how paper could be brilliant. "So what did you write?"

"Oh, lots of stuff. It was late at night, I really don't remember."

"But you asked about the diary? I mean, that she should send it?"

She stopped walking. "You don't believe me, do you?"

"I believe you," I said carefully. "But I think I'd like to see the letter. I mean, because it's my project too, right?"

"Of course. But it's already in the envelope. Sealed."

"Well, we can unseal it, can't we?"

"Fine," Francesca said, frowning. "If you insist."

She unbuttoned a pocket of her zebra jacket and handed me a small, stamped envelope the color of spearmint Trident.

Aug 28

A little past midnite

Dearest greatest Greatest-grandma Isabel,

How are things in San Fran? Is yr hip any better? Does yr new nurse speak louder? I hope so!!!

I'm extremely well. I LOVE staying with Aunt Sam its so much better than Montblanc Academy which was an utter catastrophy, did Dad tell you? I miss Daddy desprately of course but NOT Saudi AT ALL. Mom is in Paris now, did you know that? She e-mailed Aunt Sam about a new ahem friend so maybe we'll be invited for a spring weding but qui sais? School is a deadly bore as usuall, all the teachers are useless except for History, she's desperately in love with the Art teacher. The kids here are what yd expect normal and completely smug they have NO CONCEPT of the real world, or anyway life beyond Blanton, I do have one good friend tho. The rabbits are a bloody pain in the you know what, how is Snowball?

PLEASE write back!!!
Lovelovelove,
    Frankie
    PS!!! Do you rember Angelica's diary in yr attick? The earthquake one, can you send it, please? Ask Uncle Teddy to find it, I'm sure he knows where it is. Kisses, ily, thanx!!

I handed it back, feeling incredibly ashamed of myself. Angelica Beaumont was real, her sister Isabel was real, and Francesca had written a real letter. Her writing was worse than Ashley Scavullo's, which meant I'd better type up the project myself, but I was sort of expecting I'd have to, anyway. "Sorry about your mom," I said, only because I couldn't think what else to say.

"What for?" she asked, not looking at me.

"I don't know. Because she's in Paris."

"Evie," Francesca said. "Please. Living in Paris is not so bloody tragic."

"I meant—"

"I know what you meant. And I'm utterly fine with her living wherever she wants. I don't even *like* veggie burgers."

"What? I wasn't talking about veggie burgers."

"No, actually I think you were," she said, fixing the button on her collar. Then suddenly she changed the subject. "By the way. Did you notice the stationery?"

"Not really."

She handed me the letter again. "Look at the top. The monogram."

I stared at it. But all I saw was <SP>. Like the towels in her aunt's bathroom. "What about it?"

"SP," Francesca said patiently. "Like Espee. Samantha Pattison, Stephanie Pierce. Same initials, Evie. Isn't that such a fascinating coincidence?"

I glanced at her. "Fascinating in what way?"

"Oh, we haven't figured that out yet," she answered, smiling.

chapter 9

When we got to school, Lily and Nisha were sitting on the grass. Lily was talking to Can You Please Pass the Syrup, but as soon as we plopped down, he got up and ran away.

"You okay?" Lily asked me immediately. "Hi, Francesca."

"Okay about what?" Francesca asked cheerfully.

"Nothing," I muttered. "It's totally unimportant."

"Well," Lily said. "Actually, Evie. Something just happened, but Nisha says you probably don't want to hear it."

I pretend-smiled. "Yeah? Then I probably don't."

"It's about Evie's crush, isn't it?" Francesca asked. They

stared at her. "Didn't she tell you? I'm psychic about these things."

"Psychic," Nisha repeated. "Right." She turned her back to Francesca and rolled her eyes at me. "Gaby's telling everyone that Kayla and you-know-who are going out."

"Okay," I said.

"*Okay?* Your heart is being smashed like an empty soda can and that's all you can say about it?"

"Shut up, Neesh," Lily scolded. She looked at me with best-friend eyes. "Listen, Evie, we're totally here for you. So if you want to talk—"

"Thanks."

"But maybe now isn't the best time." She blinked once in the direction of Francesca, who was adjusting her faux-fur collar.

"Actually," I said slowly, "Francesca knows the whole thing. Not that there's anything to know."

Nisha's eyes flashed. "Um, Evie? Can I talk to you a minute? In private?"

I followed her to the big maple tree in front of the building.

"Okay," she said in a small, pinched voice. "Francesca knows *about Zane*?"

I nodded.

"How?"

"I'm not sure. She kind of just figured it out."

"Because she's psychic, right?" Nisha shook her head. "How could you do that, Evie? Not talking to us, but telling *Francesca*?"

"I didn't tell her anything," I insisted. "And anyway, Nisha, however she knows about it, it's not such a terrible thing."

"Meaning?"

"I don't know. I just wish you'd give her a chance. And Lily, too."

She gaped at me. "Oh, excellent. So we're the problem here?"

"That's not what I said."

"You said—okay, *implied*—we're being mean to Francesca. Who suddenly knows your deepest, innermost feelings. Unlike your two best friends, who you've completely shut out."

"I'm really sorry," I said in a tight voice. "I don't mean to shut you out. It's just that I'm not really comfortable talking about the Zane situation."

"Yeah, we've noticed. How come?"

"I don't know. Because it's embarrassing. And you guys won't leave me alone about it."

"But you *are* comfortable sharing it with Francesca, right? *Why?*"

You know how when you break a glass, it shatters all over the floor? It felt like there were a majillion glass bits in my throat. "I'm not sharing it with Francesca. I swear."

"She's such a fake. I know you think she's so cool and fun and sophisticated —"

"Just shut up, Nisha. Please." Now my eyes were starting to sting. "Okay, you want to hear the truth? I'm really, really upset about Zane. I feel exactly like what you said, a smashed-up empty soda can. And I can't *also* deal with all this jealousy about Francesca."

She flinched. "Oh. And that's what you think this is about? Jealousy?"

I bit my lip to keep it from trembling. "Yes," I said softly. "I do."

"You don't know anything, Evie," she said in a choky voice.

And she turned and ran across the grass to Lily.

By Morning Homeroom there were three big news stories circulating on the seventh-grade Hard Team: KAYLA GOING OUT

WITH ZANE! EVIE HEARTBROKEN! EVIE FIGHTS WITH BFF NISHA! It was amazing. I don't know if people were texting one another in the hallway or communicating by telepathy, but by the time I took my seat, it seemed as if everyone was totally updated. "Zane's a jerk," Katie Finberg whispered in my ear, which was a nice thing to say, I guess, even if it was completely wrong. And right before morning announcements, Gaby came over to my desk. "Hang in there," she said sweetly. "I'm sure it'll all work out with Nisha."

I waited for her to do her car-alarm laugh, but she didn't. Because she wasn't teasing; she was actually feeling *sorry* for me. And my throat was so sore from not-crying that I couldn't even answer her. Besides, even if I could, what would I say: *You're right, Gaby, this fight was meaningless?* Because how did I know that? We'd never actually fought before. (Argued, teased, annoyed, but never *fought*.) And where was Nisha, anyway? I looked around the room. She was sitting near the door with Lily, and she was all hunched over and shaking her head, while Lily was rubbing her shoulder and saying something private. When I looked at them, Lily caught my eye and smiled, but it wasn't a friendly smile or even a sympathetic smile. It was a sad smile, a you-really-hurt-Nisha's-feelings smile, as if *I* was the one who'd caused all this bad feeling. And hadn't just this morning been Crushed by a Crush, which they'd both seemed to have completely forgotten.

Right after Homeroom was Art. I just sort of sloshed my hands around in the papier-mâché juice and pretended to work, while Nisha and Lily talked quietly with Mr. Rafferty, then took stations on the opposite side of the studio. In the middle of class Espee speed-walked into the studio and whispered something to Mr. Rafferty. I could tell that Francesca was bugging out her eyes and grinning at me, but I kept my head down and acted like I didn't even notice.

The rest of the morning was boring and normal and totally endless, although the good news was that I never had to sit LilyEvieNisha and have them ignore me, which would have been just about unbearable. But at lunch I had to make a quick decision: Was I going to avoid Nisha and Lily and sit with (for example) Francesca? Or was I going to plop myself down next to my two best friends and apologize, even though I couldn't figure out what to apologize for?

The truth was, I really, really wanted to apologize, because I needed all this bad feeling to go away. Immediately. And I guess I could have made some kind of generic comment like, "I'm sorry I hurt your feelings," or, "I'm sorry we had a fight." But something inside me just couldn't do it. If Lily and Nisha were my best friends, I told myself, they'd realize how hurt I was, and how unfair they were being. About Francesca. And the Attic Project. And Zane. And of course me. Apologizing would be like saying none of it even mattered. But it did.

So instead of going to the cafeteria and apologizing (or not-apologizing), I found myself doing a very weird thing: I knocked on Espee's door. Not to talk about any of this, but just to have her look at me with her calm, pale, incredibly smart eyes. (I didn't even need a sparkle; I just needed a normal look.) This was her lunch period too; I knew that from a couple of days ago, when we'd begged to be a trio.

"Come in," she called in a friendly voice, so I opened the door and walked into her room.

She was sitting at her cluttered desk, eating straw-berry yogurt and listening to some faraway-sounding New Age music. It was funny how the music made it seem like this wasn't even a classroom, like I was walking into her own private boudoir. Which was, by the way, the complete opposite of Samantha Pattison's, all crammed with books and spidery plants and exotic-looking travel posters. COME TO EXCITING ANDALUSIA, one of them said, and I thought: *How exactly did Espee wind up in this (as Francesca put it) dreary little suburb? Did she see a poster that said COME TO EXCITING BLANTON? And took it literally?*

And did she really have a deep, dark secret that was keeping her here?

Was Francesca right?

"Evie," Ms. Pierce said, staring right into my face. "Everything okay?"

"Yes! I just wanted to ask about the San Francisco Earthquake. I was wondering if you could recommend some secondary sources for my Attic Project."

Phew, I thought. *That sounded like English.*

She put down her plastic spoon. "Oh, yes. You're working with Francesca. How's that going?"

"Great."

"That's wonderful. I had a feeling you two would be an excellent team. I guess all you needed was a little push."

"Excuse me?"

"Well, you know, teachers chat about their students. The way students chat about their teachers." She smiled as if we were sharing some kind of private, juicy secret. *DO*

NOT BLUSH, I yelled at myself. "And what I heard from Mr. Womack was that you were in a bit of a rut last year. I mean socially."

"He said that?" Now I was definitely blushing. Because how could he say that about me? If anybody was in a rut, it was Mr. Womack. *The Legacy of Ancient This. The Legacy of Ancient That*—

"Anyway," she said sweetly, "I'm glad it's all working out for you. And I can't wait to see your Attic Project. Now, about the earthquake."

She got up from her desk and walked to the back wall of her classroom where there was a giant bookcase. Then she started taking down a whole bunch of old-looking books. "Here's a good one, here's one that has several excellent photos, here's one you should get a copy of from the school library—"

The whole time she was talking, her back was to me. And suddenly I did a terrible thing.

I'm not sure why. Maybe I was just so crazed from everything that had happened this morning. Maybe I was upset about the "little bit of a rut" comment. Maybe I was curious about the so-called deep, dark secret. Maybe all of the above.

Anyway, whatever the reason, this is what happened: I peeked at Espee's computer screen.

Which said:

O my darling, how I wish I could look into your eyes and express my truest feelings. But cruel fate has come between us . . .

chapter 10

As soon as Francesca took her seat next to me in Spush, I grabbed her arm. "I have to tell you something," I said in this squeaky helium-voice. "Can you meet me at dismissal? In front of the school?"

"Of course." She scrunched her forehead at me. "Are you all right?"

"Yes. No."

Then Nisha and Lily sat down and started whispering to each other, so I opened my Spush notebook and blindly copied what Espee was writing on the whiteboard: *Life, Liberty, and the Pursuit of Happiness.* By the time I finished writing the word "happiness," I could tell that Nisha was peeking at me. So I tried to give her a serious smile, not an everything's-cool-what-a-nice-day smile, which would have been totally fake, obviously. But all she did was turn away and slump into her seat. *Well, at least I tried*, I told myself, not that it made me feel any better. And I would have tried again, except she avoided eye contact for the entire period.

When school was finally over for the day, I sat on the front steps waiting for Francesca, my mind scampering around like Topaz or Tourmaline. All of a sudden, someone was sitting next to me.

And it wasn't Francesca. It was Zane. Wait, let me rephrase that: IT WAS ZANE.

"Oh! Hi," I sputtered. "How are you?"

"Not bad." He squinted at the sun. "Man, it's hot. You know what that means?"

"Global warming?"

"No. Well, probably." He did that head-jerk thing with his bangs. "I just meant the place will be mobbed."

"What place?"

He made an are-you-kidding-me face. "My dad's? I Scream for Ice Cream?"

"Oh, right," I said brilliantly. "But that's good, isn't it? I mean, for business."

"Sure. But it also means I have to work this afternoon." He blinked his almost-amber-colored eyes. "So will you be coming in for the usual?"

"The what?"

"What you always get. Single scoop of chocolate chip in a sugar cone."

My heart skittered in my chest. *Omigod,* I yelled at myself. *Omigod. He actually notices what I order!*

Then again, I do it like twelve majillion times a week.

"I might," I said vaguely. "I've actually got a ton of homework. For Espee."

"What about your friends?"

Uh, wrong question right now. "Actually, they've got the same homework as me."

"Too bad," he said, patting my shoulder exactly two times. "Well, good luck with all that. See ya, Evie."

Then he stood and walked off to join the jersey-wearers.

My heart was still skittering when Francesca showed up maybe four seconds later. "Was that Zane?" she asked, out of breath.

I nodded. "He was just advertising. For his dad's store. Don't smile."

"I wouldn't dream of it." She stared right into my face. "He likes you, Evie."

"He definitely does *not*."

"You're wrong. I can tell these things, remember?" She sat down next to me. "So why were you acting so strange before in Spush?"

"Shh!" I grabbed Francesca's arm again. "If I tell you, you have to promise not to tell anybody. I mean it."

"Who would I tell?"

"That's not the point, Francesca. You have to promise."

Her eyes looked serious. "Okay, I promise."

"I think you're right about Espee," I blurted out. "I saw this passionate love letter she was writing. On her computer."

"You hacked into her computer?"

"*No*. Of course not! I read it by accident. Well, actually, I read it on purpose, but I didn't know I'd be reading *that*."

She nodded. "What did it say?"

"I don't know. 'O my darling, how I wish I could look into your eyes and express my truest feelings. But cruel fate has come between us.'"

"'CRUEL FATE?'"

"Yeah. Cruel fate. Keep your voice down, okay?"

"Whoops. Sorrysorrysorry. What do you suppose she means by 'cruel fate'?"

"Who knows?" I looked across the grass to the faculty parking lot. Teachers were getting into their cars and driving off for the weekend. It was so bizarre to think of them having actual messed-up love lives. Especially Espee.

"Hmm," said Francesca. "All right, Evie, so let's think this through. What 'cruel fate' could possibly keep her away from gorgeous Theo?" Her eyes lit up. "I know! Maybe the school has some kind of boring rule about teacher romance."

"The message didn't say anything about Theo Rafferty," I reminded her. "It could have been to anyone."

"Evie," Francesca said, her voice rising dangerously. "Do you really think this letter was to her pet *rabbit*?"

"Of course not! But maybe she has another boyfriend somewhere."

"I seriously doubt that. You saw the way she looks at him."

"No, I didn't. *You* saw it."

"Right. I did." Francesca sighed. "Poor, poor Espee. How absolutely tragic!"

"We don't know that it's tragic," I protested. "We don't know anything."

"Oh, please. Don't be so paralyzed, Evie! We know more than enough."

Before I could ask her what she meant by that, she stood up, reached for my arm, and pulled me up too.

That was when I felt something shift inside my backpack, like a small avalanche. Espee's books. Somehow, with all the craziness today, I'd totally forgotten about them. But of course I couldn't forget. I couldn't *let* myself forget.

"Listen, Francesca," I said nervously. "Speaking of Espee. We really, really need to start working on the Attic Project this weekend."

"Well, we can't." She took off her zebra jacket and fanned herself. "How can we? We don't even have the diary yet."

"We can still do research. Espee gave me a ton of books today."

"Oh, really? What on?"

I stared at her. "The San Francisco Earthquake, obviously. That's what the project is *about*, isn't it?"

Francesca scrunched up her nose. "I'm not personally enthralled with the whole research aspect, to be honest with you. I prefer to think about actual human beings. So if you don't mind, Evie, I'll just concentrate on Angelica Beaumont."

I could feel my throat getting tight. "How *can* you when there's nothing to concentrate *on*?"

"Well, we'll be getting the diary soon enough. And, anyway, I can't possibly do any research this weekend. I'm going to the shore."

"What shore? You mean the beach?"

"It's a family tradition. Labor Day weekend at our beautiful, beloved beach house. Actually, it's the perfect chance to snoop about Angelica."

"You mean like in the *ocean*?"

"Don't be so sarcastic. There'll be tons of relatives there. Somebody will know something." Then she gave me her dazzling smile. "Maybe you can join us."

"Yeah. I really don't think so."

"Oh, come on, Evie. You desperately need to get out of Blanton. *Especially* this weekend. Ask your mom if you can, okay?"

"Francesca."

"Just ask."

A few minutes later we were at our two houses. I went inside mine, dropping my earthquake-book-heavy backpack on the kitchen floor. "Mom?" I called. "Mom?" I was positive she'd be off bulldozing mudrooms with Caroline,

but to my shock, she was home, sitting in our freezingly
air-conditioned living room, staring at her laptop. And not
on her cell for once.

"Evie," she said as soon as I walked into the living room.
She closed her laptop and frowned at me. "Are you feeling
all right? You look pale, honey."

"I feel pale," I said weakly. "Maybe I should go to the
beach this weekend."

"The beach?"

"With Francesca. She invited me." I flopped down on
the loveseat. "It's a family tradition. We'll be doing research
for our history project."

To me it sounded like a lie. Or a joke. But weirdly enough,
Mom wasn't laughing. "What about Nisha and Lily?"

"I think they're busy. On their own project."

"The entire Labor Day weekend?"

I sighed. "It's a major assignment. For Ms. Pierce. You
remember how crazy she made Grace."

Mom pretended I hadn't said that. "Well, good for
Nisha and Lily. I mean for working so hard. Grades are so
important, Evie."

"I know."

"Because look at your sister. She wants to go to a top-tier college, but they're all so competitive these days. And don't think that just because you're in middle school—"

"I don't," I said quickly. Because I knew this speech by heart. And once Mom got started on the subject of Why Humans Need Straight A's, it was hard for her to stop. "My grades are fine, Mom. They always are."

"Oh, of course. I'm just saying." I could see the worry lines between her eyebrows start to fade. Not totally disappear, though. "Okay, so what are you telling me, Evie? You've become buddies with Francesca now?"

"She's just my partner." I shrugged. "I barely know her."

"But you want to spend the weekend together. Well, I'll certainly need a few more details. Like what beach we're even discussing."

"You mean I *can*?"

"Why not?" She smiled tiredly. "Grace wants to visit some colleges, and that'll be a bore for you. And it'll be good for you to get away. You've been so stressed lately."

I jumped up and gave her a gigantic hug. "Thanks," I said. "Really, Mom."

"Glad that I'm not being *unfair* for once," she teased. Then her cell phone rang. So she patted my butt and walked off into the kitchen, doing her Delightful Voice.

chapter 11

While Mom was on her cell talking over the details with Samantha Pattison, I stuffed my backpack for the weekend: two tanks, extra pair of shorts, underwear, flip-flops, flower-patterned bathing suit that sort of camouflaged my chest, Lily's too-big San Diego Zoo T-shirt for sleeping, Spush notebook, earthquake books. Plus sunscreen, lip gloss, and my cell. Plus pens and my toothbrush and three packs of Bubblelicious, in case I got carsick. Or nervous. For a second I thought about taking my amber-mosquito necklace, but it was too precious to risk losing in the ocean. So I left it in my desk drawer. For safekeeping.

Early Saturday morning, Dad stopped me at the door. "So you were just planning to run out? Not even a good-bye kiss?"

"Sorry," I said quickly. "I thought you guys were asleep."

"Even if we were," he answered, giving me a big hug that smelled like sleep. Then he looked in my eyes. "Have a little fun at the beach, kiddo. Don't be nuts about schoolwork like your sister."

From his bathrobe pocket his BlackBerry made a wind-chime noise. He took it out and groaned as he read the screen.

"Don't *you* be nuts about work-work," I teased. "And enjoy Grace's colleges!"

"Yeah, I'll certainly try," he muttered, typing something and shuffling into the kitchen.

"And we're OFF," shouted Francesca as the black convertible screeched down the driveway. "Here we come, beach! YEEE-HAW!"

"Okay, girls, but put on sunhats," said Samantha Pattison, who was wearing a pink Florida Marlins cap and these huge actressy sunglasses. "Or you'll both scorch before we get there."

"Don't worry, we won't!" Francesca answered. "We're *dripping* with sunscreen. And besides, we want to feel the wind in our hair! Don't we, Evie?"

"Sure!" I said. My mouth was grinning so much, it was hard to talk, especially over the hot wind.

Samantha turned on a country CD by some singer I'd never heard of, and then she started singing along in a beautiful alto voice that sounded like warm honey. (The whooshing car-air was so noisy, I couldn't hear exactly what she was singing, but it sounded like, 'Baby, this something pain in my something.') Pretty soon Francesca joined in, mostly off-key, and then finally I did, even though I didn't know any words. As soon as the CD was finished, Samantha popped in another, and then another, and we just kept speeding up the thruway singing our lungs out, with the wind snapping our hair in our faces. *Yippee,* I yelled to myself. *Bye-bye, Blanton! For three whole days!*

Finally, we were there. Or rather, a mile from there. When we got to a curvy little path sprinkled with beach sand, Samantha made us get out of the car and brush our hair. We watched her put on some glossy pale pink lipstick and stretch her mouth, as if she were about to go onstage. And then we got back in the car and drove up to the beach house, which was maybe the weirdest-looking place I'd ever seen. In my *life*.

Because it wasn't just one house. It looked like four different teeny houses scotch-taped together: a gray-shingled bungalow attached to an ultra-modern glass room on one side and a run-down-looking white ranch on the other. The second story looked like something straight out of Blanton: much newer, painted in a color Mom liked to call "eggshell," with huge, curvy windows and a little balcony. And then the garage, which was separate from the house, basically looking like a damp cardboard box just big enough to store two cars and a lawn mower.

"Well? What do you think?" asked Francesca, her eyes shining.

Before I could answer, two incredibly freckled, Mom-aged women came racing out of the house wearing serious navy blue bathing suits and no shoes.

"Frankie!" they shrieked. "Sammy! What took you so long!"

"Traffic," Samantha lied, stepping gracefully out of the driver's seat. Francesca leaped out of the back and started hugging the freckled women. And then two men, one sunburnt, the other with an enormous belly, came out of the house demanding hugs of their own.

I wasn't sure what to do so I just stayed in the car and watched.

"Evie! Come over here!" Francesca ordered. "Meet Aunt Bitsy, Aunt Beebee, Uncle Croy, and Uncle Gib." I took a breath and walked over to them and shook every-body's hand. *Omigod,* I thought. *How am I supposed to remember who's who? They don't even have real names!* I looked them over frantically, trying to think of how to tell them apart.

Aunt Yellowteeth gave me an enormous smile. "We're so pleased you could make it, Evie. Frankie's told us so much about you."

She had? "Well, thanks for inviting me. We're really psyched about our project."

"What project?" Uncle Big Belly demanded.

"Oh, it's nothing. Just for school," Francesca said. "We'll tell you about it later."

"You bet later," Uncle Sunburnt said, smiling. "This is supposed to be a vacation, young lady."

"So where's Quentin?" Francesca asked, grabbing her bag from the car.

"He's down at the shore waiting for you," Aunt Ponytail answered. "With Timmybear, who we're supposed to call Timmy, now that he's started second grade."

"Quentin?" I asked Francesca as I lifted my own backpack.

"My cousin. Fourteen. Staggeringly immature, but c'est la vie. Ooh, Evie, let's see if we can have my favorite bedroom!"

She sprinted down the hallway to the ultra-modern side of the house, where two cots were set up in the middle of a room so empty, it could have been a closet. (Not Samantha's, obviously—I mean a normal closet.) But the amazing thing was that it had enormous windows facing the water, and if you stood on a cot and looked out (which Francesca did, and which she made me do too), it almost felt as if you were out on the ocean.

"Mother Darling loves this room," Francesca said happily. "She says it makes her feel as if she's on a fabulous cruise ship."

"You mean your mom comes here?"

"Once in a great while. She says it's the only place in the States where she feels peaceful. Of course, to be peaceful, it has to be empty. Meaning no relatives." She picked up a clamshell from a small table dividing the two cots. "She found this on the beach a few winters ago. It's utterly boring, but for some reason I like it. Isn't that odd?"

"It's very nice," I said. Even though, frankly, it was your basic normal clamshell.

Five minutes later we were in our suits and running down to the shore to join Quentin and Timmy. Timmy was just a little kid, but Quentin looked kind of like an eighth-grade jersey-wearer (except of course he was wearing swimming trunks). Immediately Francesca grabbed Quentin's boogie board, and she and Timmy headed out for the waves, laughing and yelling these dorky pirate expressions. So then Quentin and I took after them, yelling even stupider taunts and splashing like crazy. We had a giant ridiculous sea battle until the water got black and freezing and Timmy's lips started turning blue. And when we came inside the house, shivering and tired and dripping sand all over the kitchen, Quentin touched my elbow. "That was fun, Evie," he said, and I grinned back at him because it really, really was.

"Don't you just love it here?" Francesca said, looking up at the stars. We were on the beach, a few yards from the Pattison house, lying on a moth-eaten afghan that Aunt

Ponytail had crocheted. It was about two hours after we'd finished an enormous dinner of fried chicken, corn on the cob, biscuits, and raspberry pie, and my shorts still couldn't close at the top button.

"It's perfect," I said truthfully. I looked up at the stars and started counting the ones on Orion's belt. Almost everything that had been freaking me out recently—the fight with Nisha and Lily, the smashed-up soda can business with Zane—seemed far away that night. And I knew we'd be making progress on the Attic Project that weekend, so I wasn't even stressed about that, for a change.

Francesca sighed. "I wish I could stay here forever."

I stopped counting. "You mean like live here? And go to school?"

"Oh, forget about school. School is not the whole wide world. And neither is boring Blanton." She rolled on her side and looked at me. "Evie, don't you ever think about bigger things?"

"Like what?"

"Oh, I don't know. Cosmos questions. Like whether the stars control our destiny. Or if everything in the universe is utterly random."

"Everything?"

"Not *everything*, maybe. I mean the truly important things. Like love."

I laughed. "Actually, Francesca, that kind of question never crosses my mind."

"How tragic," she said sympathetically. "Okay, so think about it now. Do you believe in soulmates?"

"Soulmates?"

"You know. Like Cathy and Heathcliff in *Wuthering Heights*."

I shrugged. "I've never read that book, Francesca. I looked at it the other day, but it's just so . . . wordy."

"Of course it's wordy. It's a *book*," she said, laughing. Then she sat up and added casually, "Speaking of gorgeous words. Can I tell you this absolutely epic idea I had? Remember that letter you read on Espee's computer yesterday?"

"Uh, sure."

"Well, Evie. What do you think would happen if Theo Rafferty actually received it? Don't you think it would be like this massive lightning bolt in their relationship? And then her life would change. Both of their lives. Happily ever after."

"Francesca?" Now I sat up too. "What are you talking about?"

"I bet you anything she'd never send it to him. On her own. So then I started thinking: What if somebody else—"

The raspberry pie took a weird turn in my stomach. "Did what?"

"You know. Sent it to him somehow."

I almost choked. "Are you psychotic? That's the worst idea I ever heard in my life!"

"What's wrong with it?"

"What's *wrong*? Well, for one thing, it's totally dishonest."

"How is it dishonest? We wouldn't be making anything up. We'd just be sending along her exact words."

"Which maybe she doesn't *want*."

"Why wouldn't she? You think she's happy? All alone with her ice cream every night?"

I almost laughed. "First of all, you don't even know if she sent it herself. Maybe she e-mailed it."

"Of course she didn't *e-mail* it. You don't *e-mail* someone a *love letter*. You write it on really beautiful stationery."

"And, anyway, maybe she *hates* ice cream. Maybe she's *ecstatic* with her life."

"Oh, please. You read what she wrote. 'Cruel fate.' If she's truly so ecstatic, then why would she call it that?"

"I don't know," I admitted. "Besides, haven't you ever written some crazy, stupid thing you didn't want anybody to see?"

"No," said Francesca. "Why would I? That would just be a bloody waste of time." She plopped back down on the blanket. "Oh, never mind! It was just an idea I had. Forget I even mentioned it."

"Gladly."

"All right, then. Sorry."

I sat there in the dark, listening to the waves crash.

"It's just that I feel so desperately *sorry* for Espee," Francesca blurted out. "She's such a tragic person, don't you think? Stuck in that miserable little school, wearing those horrible pants. Assigning those deadly boring research papers to kids who think she's a witch."

I shrugged. Then I poked my finger in the sand and started drawing nervous circles.

She reached across the blanket to touch my arm. "Evie, can I tell you something personal? I just feel sometimes as if I have this amazing *understanding* of things. It's like a gift I have, you know? To know what people truly want. And that makes me want to *help* them."

"Francesca," I said, trying to sound calm and normal and

in control. "This is really not about your so-called psychic powers."

"Don't say 'so-called.' That sounds as if you don't believe me!"

"I'm not saying that. It's just incredibly not the *point*."

She frowned. "Okay, you're angry. Please, please, please don't be."

"Just promise me you won't send Espee's love note."

"If you insist," she said, pretending to laugh. "Are we okay now?"

"I guess."

"Well, lovely, then." All of a sudden she got up from the blanket and ran into the beach house.

For a few minutes I sat there shivering, looking up at the stars. But it made no sense to stay out on the beach all by myself, so finally I got up, brushed the sand off my legs, and followed her inside.

chapter 12

The next morning at breakfast, Francesca shocked me again.

"Yarrr," Quentin said as he squirted maple syrup on a stack of French toast. "Shiver me timbers. I challenge ye guys to a second sea battle. This very morn."

"We can't," Francesca said impatiently. "We're busy."

"We are?" I glanced quickly at Quentin. In the morning light you could see that he had fuzz on his upper lip. And a tan under the freckles on his cheeks, and wavy brownish hair. He wasn't Zane-level cute, but he wasn't deformed, either. And he was nice. And also *not* immature, whatever Francesca meant by that, anyway.

Francesca grabbed a box of Corn Flakes from the messy counter and poured herself a huge bowl. "Well, obviously, Evie. We have all that research for the Attic Project. You're going to read those books and I'm going to investigate Angelica."

"You mean you'll be doing homework *all day*?" Quentin hooted. "Then what was the point of coming here, Frankie?"

"So I can interview my relatives," she answered seriously.

I watched Francesca dump almost a full pint of blueberries over her Corn Flakes, and I thought: *What exactly is going on here? Why does she suddenly care so much about the Attic Project? Is it because last night I freaked out when she talked about the love letter? Well, maybe it's okay that I freaked out. That's not such a terrible thing, actually.*

"You know what?" I said enthusiastically. "We can take the earthquake books down to the beach. As long as we don't get them sandy."

Francesca nodded. Her hair fell into her cereal bowl, and she didn't even push it back.

After breakfast we put on our dampish bathing suits and walked down to the ocean, lugging a blanket, the earthquake books, and also our Spush spiral notebooks. We spread the blanket carefully, then each took a book from the pile and started reading. My hands were greasy from sunscreen, but I managed to grip my pen tightly and take pages and pages of fascinating notes, all about San Francisco life right before the earthquake hit. And I even managed to tune out Quentin and Timmy, who were boogie boarding nearby and yelling, "Avast, ye scurvy dogs," and other dorky pirate expressions.

The whole time, Francesca hardly said a word. She just kept reading her book, once in a while writing in her spiral notebook. Considering how long it had taken for her to focus on our project, I didn't exactly want to interrupt her. But after an hour or so the un-Francesca silence was really starting to get to me.

"So," I said finally, "do you know if Angelica lived on Nob Hill?"

"What?" She looked up.

"A ton of mansions were destroyed on Nob Hill," I said, pointing to a photo in my book. "You said she lived in a mansion. Do you know the address?"

"No, I don't," she said, frowning. "I'll ask my relatives about that after lunch."

"We don't have to do this the entire day, you know."

"Oh, I know." She squinted toward the sparkling ocean. "Okay if I go for a swim?"

"Of course! You don't need my permission!"

"I wasn't asking," she said, her face breaking into a grin. "I was just being disgustingly polite."

I grinned back at her. Whatever weird feeling was left over from last night was suddenly gone now, and I was glad. I watched her jog into the ocean and tackle Timmy from behind. Then I opened her spiral notebook, just to take a quick peek. This is what she'd been writing:

SF EQ
4/18/1906
5:12 am
SPUSH
SPUSH
Spushhhhhh . . . .
Stephanie Pierce
Stephanie Pierce Rafferty
Ms. Stephanie Pierce-Rafferty
History is a story
History is a story
we tell ourselves

Life liberty the pursuit of
happily
      ever
         after

"Hey there, scalawag," said a teasing voice. "Making progress?"

Horrified, I shut the notebook. "Hi, Quentin. Yes, we are."

"Cool. Then come battle."

I nodded. "In a minute. Can I ask you something first?"

"Sure." He squatted on the blanket and looked at me curiously.

"Um, maybe it's none of my business," I said. "But do you know why Francesca was kicked out of that other school?"

"Not really. Something about a paper she wrote. Or didn't write, I forget which. Frankie's never been much of a student. Even though she's been to a ton of schools."

"She has? Why?"

"Well, she's kind of lived all over." He shaded his eyes, and we both watched Francesca lift Timmy out of the water and then toss him back in, squealing. "I never heard the whole story from my mom. But Frankie's family is unbelievably messed up, that's all I *do* know."

"You mean her mom?"

"Both of them. Her dad's, like, totally obsessed with his job and making money, even though they're seriously loaded. And her mom's like, *Frankie who? You mean I have a daughter somewhere?* And now she's living with Aunt Sam, who's pretty much off in her own world."

"Hey, Samantha's okay," I argued, thinking about the amazing way she sang in the car. She still seemed to me kind of silly and poofy, but she was also obviously incredibly talented. And really, how could you memorize all those sad, painful songs without having a sensitive heart?

I suddenly realized Quentin was staring at me.

"Yeah, I guess she's cool," he was saying. "But not the parent type, maybe. Anyway, Frankie has a best friend now, so everybody's happy." He grabbed my arm and starting dragging me into the ocean. "Come on, Evie. I challenge thee to a rematch sea battle, thou miserable lowly wench."

"Angelica who?" Aunt Yellowteeth demanded as she passed the potato salad.

"Beaumont," Francesca answered. "Great-grandma Isabel's big sister."

"Isabel had a sister?"

"Oh, you remember, Beebee. Teddy's aunt. The socialite suffragette," Aunt Ponytail said, winking.

"And we're doing a big research project about the 1906 earthquake," I said excitedly. "So Francesca wrote Isabel—"

"Where?" Uncle Sunburnt interrupted. "At the old address?"

"At the *usual* address," Francesca said. "The one I visited last Easter. Why? Is there a different one?"

"Since early June," Aunt Ponytail said, passing me an enormous plate of hot seashells. "Isabel moved to a nursing home, a very nice one in Sacramento. Evie, don't you want any steamers?"

"No thanks," I said politely.

"Evie only eats veggie burgers," Francesca said, not looking at me. "So who's living in her house now? Great-uncle Teddy?"

"No, he never settles in any place for too long. But I believe he's trying to sell it."

"Well, good luck to Teddy," Uncle Sunburnt snorted. "Nobody will want that creaky old thing. The energy bills alone—"

I nudged Francesca. "But your great-uncle can still get the diary, right?"

"What diary?" Quentin demanded.

Timmy started singing. "Quentin said diarrhea, Quentin said—"

"I did *not*," Quentin said, giving Timmy a noogie. "I said *diary*, you little doof. And Evie said it first." He grinned at me.

Francesca smiled. "Angelica kept a diary during the San Francisco Earthquake," she explained. "Teddy told me all about it."

I almost choked on my potato salad. "He *told* you? You mean you never actually *read* it?"

"Not personally," she answered, calmly spreading a gigantic blob of butter on her roll. "But Teddy says it's fascinating."

"I'll bet." Uncle Big Belly grinned. "Wasn't she the one with all those husbands?"

"Never mind," said Aunt Yellowteeth.

"And that secret affair with the married movie star—"

"Gib. The girls aren't asking about that."

"Oh yes, we are!" Francesca insisted. "We want to hear all the juicy details. Don't we, Evie?"

I didn't answer. I poked my potato salad with my fork.

"I thought this was supposed to be a history project," Aunt Ponytail said, smiling.

"Oh, it *is*," Francesca told her. "But we're supposed to research the whole person. To get the whole story."

"We-ell," Aunt Yellowteeth said, slowly and loudly, "under the circumstances, I really don't think Frankie needs to hear gossip and innuendo."

"Under *what* circumstances?" Samantha demanded. She'd been so quiet, I'd forgotten she was at the table. But now she was looking at Aunt Yellowteeth with blazing eyes.

"Do we really need to spell it out?" Aunt Yellowteeth replied, tilting her chin toward Francesca.

"That's enough," Aunt Ponytail said sharply. "Frankie honey, would you like some ice cream? There's chocolate chip and strawberry."

"You know, Bitsy," said Samantha, still staring at Aunt Yellowteeth, "I don't think it's necessary to treat Frankie like a baby. She knows exactly what's going on with her own mother."

"Oh, does she, Sammy? And why is that?"

"Because we *talk*," Samantha said in a dramatic stage voice. "Her understanding of the situation is *extremely mature*. Sometimes I think she's more mature than I am!"

"Well, I'll certainly agree with that," Aunt Yellowteeth said into her napkin.

"Okay, you two, now stop it!" Aunt Ponytail snapped. "Mimi's relationships are her own business, and not the sort of thing we should be discussing at the table!" She scooped some strawberry ice cream into a small chipped bowl and shoved it in front of Francesca.

The conversation went on and on from that point, but I tuned out most of it, because by then my head was spinning. Mostly about this: FRANCESCA HAD NEVER READ THE DIARY. Why had I thought she had? Had she ever specifically *said* she'd read it, or was that something I'd just assumed? "Uncle Teddy" had read it, but who was he? And also *where* was he, and would he rescue the diary before Isabel's house was sold? Or worse, bulldozed into the ground?

And how were we supposed to research Angelica Beaumont's fascinating private life if nobody would even talk to us? We weren't asking about Francesca's mom, and it seemed crazy to me that anyone would think we were. *Excuse me, guys, but this is U.S. history,* I wanted to shout. *We're not discussing your messed-up family!*

Finally my brain slowed down and I took a peek at

Francesca. She hadn't even touched her ice cream; she was just sitting there, twirling the corners of her napkin. And when supper was finally over and Aunt Yellowteeth announced that everybody would be playing Scrabble, she leaned over to me and murmured, "Evie, we *desperately* have to get out of here."

I followed her out of the dining room through a little side door I hadn't noticed, and into the almost-moonlight. We both took off our flip-flops and started walking along the windy beach, listening to the waves crash.

For a long time we didn't talk. Finally Francesca said, "Sorry about dinner."

"It was fine."

"No, it wasn't. My family is a tad deranged." She picked up a broken clamshell. "So you're mad that I never read the diary?"

I took a deep breath of salty air. "Well, to be honest with you, Francesca, I'm really not thrilled about it. I mean, the project is due in eight days, we don't have the diary, and now who knows what it even *says*."

"Oh, don't worry about *that*! Uncle Teddy's been telling me about the diary *forever*. I feel as if I have the whole thing memorized. It'll be staggering once we get it, you'll see."

"Well, I hope so," I said doubtfully. "But when exactly will we have it?"

"I'll e-mail him as soon as we get home tomorrow. I'll tell him to overnight it, the very second he gets to Isabel's. So we'll definitely have it in time to write an utterly brilliant project."

What could I possibly say to all that? "Okay, then. Great."

She smiled, almost shyly. "So we're good, Evie, right?"

"Sure. I guess."

"Well, that's a huge relief!"

We walked some more. My toes were starting to get numb from the freezing tide and my eyes were stinging from the salty wind. The truth was, I wanted to go back to the house and play Scrabble or just start packing for tomorrow's trip home, but Francesca seemed to be having fun picking up shells, examining them carefully, and then tossing them as far as she could into the roaring waves.

Finally, though, she plopped onto the sand and patted a space next to her for me to sit. "Evie?" she said sweetly. "Can we talk about something? And you won't freak out or be absolutely furious?"

"I'll try," I said, suddenly aware of a prickly feeling in my stomach. "What is it?"

"All right, this is a true confession. Are you ready?"

"No."

"I'll tell you anyway. Here goes: I sent Espee's letter to Theo."

"You . . . *what*?"

"I wrote it out on nice paper, and then I mailed it. 'O my darling, truest feelings, cruel fate.' Exactly what you quoted from her computer."

"Omigod."

"I used her printy handwriting. You'd never know the difference, Evie. And I signed it Stephanie Pierce."

"Francesca. You *didn't*."

"No, I did."

"Oh, God. Oh, God."

"Okay, you're furious at me, aren't you?"

I couldn't talk. Finally, after maybe twenty seconds, I asked, "When did you send it?"

"Friday night. Right before we came here."

"So last night, when we were talking about this, when you *promised* me, you'd already—?"

"I didn't know you'd think it was a bad idea! I thought you'd actually be happy!"

"Why would you possibly think *that*?"

"Because you read Espee's computer screen! Why would you, if you didn't care about her personal life? And why would you *tell* me about it if deep down you didn't want something amazing to happen?"

I stared at the goosebumps on my arms. "Listen, Francesca. Even if I wanted something to happen, even if I thought it would be a great idea, I wouldn't just *do* it."

"I know," she said seriously. "And that makes me so sad for you."

I looked up at the stars, which seemed different from last night, as if they'd all shifted over two spaces. Everything was off somehow. I couldn't even find Orion's belt.

"Evie," Francesca begged. "Please, please, *please* don't hate me for this. I truly feel we've done an incredibly wonderful thing. A *helpful* thing. For two beautiful soulmates."

"Maybe," I answered in a tight voice. "I really just need to think about this, okay? Can we please go back to the house now?"

"Oh, absolutely." She stood up and tossed one last shell into the ocean. "Of course we can. We'll do anything you want."

chapter 13

The whole ride home, we didn't sing. Or talk very much, either, come to think of it. Just before we'd left, Samantha had had a loud whisper-fight with Aunt Yellowteeth in the run-down-looking ranch part of the house, and I could tell she was still really upset about that. And Aunt Ponytail had taken Francesca upstairs to the fancy Blanton-looking floor and said a lot of nice things about how much Francesca's mom loved her, but how "complicated" families could be sometimes. (I heard about this because Quentin had listened by the door, and then come downstairs to tell me about it while I was packing. "What's so complicated about *families*?" he'd snorted.) I knew Aunt Ponytail had said all that stuff to make Francesca feel better, but she hardly said a word once we were packed up and on the road. And of course I couldn't talk about the love letter in front of Samantha, so I spent most of the trip home staring out the window, worrying.

When we finally got back to Blanton, I thanked Francesca for the weekend, and Samantha, too, and helped carry their bags inside. ("You poor little things, did you miss us?" Samantha shouted at the rabbits, who scampered away.) And then I dragged my stuff into my own house, which seemed sane and safe and normal, even though Mom didn't put down her cell when she gave me a welcome-home hug, and Grace immediately shouted down the hallway that she was studying for the SAT, so could I please keep it down?

"Keep what down?" I asked.

"Whatever you're doing," she growled.

I stood in her doorway. "So how were your college visits?"

She groaned. "Excellent. Of course if I want to get into any of those places, I'll need ultra-perfect scores."

"No you won't, Grace," I said. "Besides, with your grades—"

"You don't know a *thing* about the college process, Evie,"

she interrupted. "Just be glad you're in seventh grade, which doesn't even *count*."

Well, it counts to me, I thought as I dumped my sandy clothes in the hamper. I was just about to go find Dad to see how he had survived three days in the car with Grumpy Grace when my cell phone rang. I didn't even have to look at the screen to know who it was.

"Evie?" Nisha was saying. "I've been calling you all weekend!"

She sounded a little anxious, louder and higher-pitched. But even so, it was just such a relief to hear her voice again.

"God, I missed you so much," I blurted out.

"Me too. So where were you, anyway?"

"At the shore with Francesca." Immediately I added, "She invited me. Her family has this fantastic old beach house."

"Oh." Nisha paused. "Well, lucky her."

"Yeah, sort of. Anyhow, it was nice to get out of Blanton." As soon as I said that, I wished I could hit the Delete key. "What about you? Did you do anything fun?"

"Hmm, let's see. You mean other than Lily making us walk Jimmy around her block four thousand times, and then being dragged by my mom to Home Depot so she could yell at the store manager for not stocking the right door hinges? You mean *excluding* all that?"

"Sorry. It doesn't sound very . . . entertaining."

"Yeah, well, don't rub it in, okay?" She sighed. "So. Since you were away I guess you haven't heard the news about Zane?"

"No." I said quickly. "What news?"

"He broke up with Kayla. Or Kayla broke up with him, depending on which version you're getting."

"That was fast."

"Yah." She waited. "You don't sound incredibly happy."

"Should I be? I mean, truthfully, Nisha, I really don't think—"

"Oh, right, I forgot, we shouldn't keep bothering you about Zane." She sighed again, sharply this time. "So just tell me about the beach, Evie. Did you get a good tan?"

"Not really. We mostly researched for our Attic Project. And we played pirates with Francesca's cousins."

"You played *pirates*? Are you, like, joking?"

"Dorky pirates. It was awesome, actually, but I guess you had to be there."

She didn't answer, and I realized I'd said that a little funny, like I was bragging I was invited to something she wasn't. And to make it okay, what I *could* have done right then was tell her about Espee's love letter, and how Francesca had sent it to Theo. But I didn't. Because judging from the way Nisha was reacting to everything, I was pretty sure she'd just start screeching an are-you-joking sort of speech, and I didn't know how to deal with it, frankly. Besides, I told myself, Francesca and I had promised each other we'd keep Espee's love life private. And whatever I thought about Francesca's own ability to keep a promise, not blabbing about the letter felt like something I owed to Espee.

So instead of all that, I just asked Nisha about her Attic Project.

"Oh, it's *awesome*," she snapped. "Well, I guess I'll see you at school tomorrow. Have a nice night."

Then she hung up on me.

That night it rained. And rained and rained, as if suddenly Mother Nature had freaked out when she realized it was September, and she hadn't been keeping up with her Autumn Project. I didn't sleep very well; I think I heard every single raindrop splatter on my windowsill. In the morning when I got out of bed the floor was so cold, I put on thick cotton socks. And for the first time in months, I went into my Serious Clothes drawer and threw on a sweater, a baggy orange one that made me look like a pumpkin.

After breakfast I rang Francesca's bell, my mind more than half made up to tell her I was quitting the Attic Project, and that I didn't want to hear one more word about Espee's *cruel fate*. As soon as she opened the door, though, it was like I just kind of lost my mental place. Francesca was wearing a yellow-and-black bumblebee scarf wound tightly around her neck, a boyish-looking white cable-knit sweater that reached her knees, red kneesocks, and the blue sparkly stilettos. On the beach she'd looked so normal; I'd totally forgotten about the costume business.

She greeted me with her dazzling smile. "Fabulous news!" she shouted as she slammed the door behind her. "I spoke to Uncle Teddy last night, and he's sending the diary!"

My heart bounced. "You mean right away?"

"Uh-huh. He's heading up there today to show the house. And he promises to overnight it first thing!"

And I told myself: *Okay, Evie, don't be stupid here. You're upset about Espee's love letter, but the Attic Project is a separate thing. Angelica's diary is finally on its way, and it's probably amazing. So why quit the project before you even*

barbara dee

get to read it? Besides, you've already done a ton of research. What sense would it make to throw it out now and have to start all over with some dorky Mystery Box?

So I just said, "Great. Tell me as soon as you get it, okay?"

"Oh, of course I will," she said, laughing. "We're partners, aren't we?"

We started walking to school, hurrying past the Scavullos' automatic sprinklers, which were thwipping around crazily, even though it had just poured all night long. And my stomach was thwipping around almost as fast, because for once I had no idea what to expect at school, and that scared me.

So to keep my mind off Theo and Espee, and all my jitters about the love letter, I did diary-math: Today was Tuesday. Say Uncle Teddy didn't actually find the diary until Wednesday, and overnighted it right away, as he'd promised. That would mean we'd have the diary on Thursday, with four days to read it and write up our report. It wasn't how I usually planned my big assignments, but it was probably doable. In the meantime I'd keep reading Espee's books, and this afternoon I'd start researching the San Francisco Earthquake online. Judging by Francesca's note-taking

get to read it? Besides, you've already done a ton of research. What sense would it make to throw it out now and have to start all over with some dorky Mystery Box?

So I just said, "Great. Tell me as soon as you get it, okay?"

"Oh, of course I will," she said, laughing. "We're partners, aren't we?"

We started walking to school, hurrying past the Scavullos' automatic sprinklers, which were thwipping around crazily, even though it had just poured all night long. And my stomach was thwipping around almost as fast, because for once I had no idea what to expect at school, and that scared me.

So to keep my mind off Theo and Espee, and all my jitters about the love letter, I did diary-math: Today was Tuesday. Say Uncle Teddy didn't actually find the diary until Wednesday, and overnighted it right away, as he'd promised. That would mean we'd have the diary on Thursday, with four days to read it and write up our report. It wasn't how I usually planned my big assignments, but it was probably doable. In the meantime I'd keep reading Espee's books, and this afternoon I'd start researching the San Francisco Earthquake online. Judging by Francesca's note-taking

150

skills, there was no point making her help me with any of this. But as long as the diary was finally on its way, she'd have plenty of Angelica-analysis to do once it arrived.

As soon as we got to school, I spotted Nisha and Lily on the grass. Nisha was laughing with Kayla and Gaby, and Lily was talking quietly to Can You Please Pass the Syrup.

"Go ahead," Francesca said cheerfully. "They're your best friends; you should hang out with them, Evie."

"Actually," I said. "Things are a little weird right now."

"What happened?"

"Nothing. Things just . . . got weird."

"That's bloody ridiculous! Friendships don't all of a sudden *just get weird*." She slipped off one of her stilettos and examined the heel.

I winced. "Um, Francesca? Can you please keep it down?"

"Eeek. Sorrysorrysorry."

She put her shoe back on and followed me over to the big maple tree where Nisha and I'd had our fight. The ground around the tree was muddy from all the rain, and I could see her skinny heels sinking into the mush.

"Things were weird this summer," I told her. "I think we all just needed a break. And now they're sort of mad about my friendship with you."

"But why would they be?" Francesca protested. "I'm not trying to pull you away from anybody!"

"I know. It's not your fault. It's more like everything I say to them is just wrong lately."

She wiped her muddy heels with a dried-up maple leaf. "Well, maybe I can fix things. What if *I* talked to them about it?"

"NO." I said it so loudly that Nisha turned around and stared at us. Then she said something to Lily, who turned around too. "I mean, really, Francesca, we have a majillion other things to worry about right now."

"Like what? I told you, we're getting the diary."

"I'm not talking about the *diary*."

She looked stumped. "Oh, you mean Espee's love letter? That's a *fabulous* thing; it's not something to *worry* about!"

"Shh!"

"Okay! But come on, Evie, aren't you excited? Or even a teeny bit curious about how he'll react?"

"Maybe a little," I admitted. "But to be honest, I'm mostly freaking out."

"Well, *don't* freak out! The problem with you—" Then Francesca gasped. "Look, look, stop talking, there she is!"

Espee was speed-walking across the grass, her hair

swinging back and forth across the shoulders of her pale gray blouse. And she had on those shapeless black pants again. It was mean and unfair to say she looked like Miss Gulch; but why, I wondered, did she always have to dress like Kansas before the tornado? Why couldn't she wear some *colors,* for a change? Why couldn't she go to Oz?

Suddenly she froze, as if she heard a sound coming from the parking lot. Then we heard it too.

"Stephie! Stephie!" a man was shouting. We spun around to see who was running toward her, waving his arms like he was trying to prevent an accident. "Steph! Stephanie! Wait!"

"Francesca," I said through my teeth. "Omigod."

She beamed. "Isn't it fantastic? Isn't it perfect? I *knew* we did the right thing! Didn't we, Evie?"

I nodded, and then I started giggling like crazy.

Because it was Theo.

chapter 14

It wasn't as if Francesca and I ever agreed, *Okay, so now the next thing is, we spy on Theo and Espee.* But I guess it just seemed to both of us like the obvious thing to do. I mean, they were like characters in a book we were writing—maybe not *Wuthering Heights*, but something romantic and passionate and not-for-little-kids. So of course we were fascinated; of course we had to know exactly what happened next. We followed them into the building and pretended to read the posters for after-school clubs while the two of them huddled in front of the faculty mailroom and talked in hushed, private voices.

Finally I couldn't stand it any longer. "Can you hear anything?" I whispered to Francesca.

"No," she whispered back. "But I'm lip-reading. Trying to. Ooh, the Sewing Club, that looks like fun," she announced in a loud, enthusiastic voice as Theo suddenly left Espee and walked past us into the main office.

I waited until he was safely inside. "What were they saying?"

Francesca shrugged. "I think she said *love*. Although it could have been *lunge*."

"Lunge? Why would she possibly—"

"No, *lunch*! They're meeting for—" Francesca pinched my elbow, because there was Theo again, coming out of the office. "On the other hand, the Bowling Club—oh, good morning, Mr. Rafferty. How was your weekend?"

He smiled. He'd gotten a tan, so his teeth looked especially white. And even whiter against his soul patch. "Very nice, thanks. And yours?"

"Highly productive."

I almost died.

Mr. Rafferty waved down the hall at a couple of math teachers. "Okay, girls, see you in Art," he said, and walked off to join them.

barbara dee

"'Highly productive'?" I whisper-screamed as soon as he couldn't hear. "I can't believe you said that!"

"Well, it was," she said, laughing. "Wouldn't you agree? Anyway, so we know they're meeting for lunch. What's your guess: his studio or Spush?"

"Spush," I said automatically. "But we can always check both."

"Yes, Evie, of course we can," Francesca said, patting my shoulder like she was saying, *Congratulations.*

The morning was a big, irrelevant blur except for Art. I told Francesca that we shouldn't hang out together in the studio, because if we started whispering or giggling during class, Theo might think we knew something. And even if there wasn't some kind of no-dating-between-teachers rule, I was pretty sure Espee would want to keep their love affair private. Which meant we needed to keep the lowest profile possible— and I didn't trust how we'd react if Espee speed-walked into the studio for a sudden middle-of-the-class rendezvous.

"Genius," Francesca murmured when I explained all this before Art. "You're right; we can't arouse suspicion. I'll do my project near the windows, you take the door."

So I took my own project—a papier-mâché ice cream

sundae—and brought it over to a work station as far from Francesca as I could get. I was just about to start painting little brown specks for chocolate chips when someone tapped my shoulder.

I nearly screamed. But it was only Lily.

"You okay, Evie?" she asked with a soft voice and worried eyes.

"Yeah. Just sort of jumpy."

She nodded. "It's because you had another fight with Nisha, right? Look, I know you're upset. But so is she."

"She's not upset, Lily. She's angry. At everything I do these days."

"Because she thinks you're dumping her. Are you?"

"Of course not!"

"Okay," Lily murmured. "Then why didn't you come over to us on the grass this morning?"

"Because yesterday Nisha hung up on me! Did she tell you that?"

"Yeah. She felt terrible about it, actually."

Not terrible enough to call back, though. "Well, after that, I didn't think she'd want a whole conversation."

Lily sighed. "Look, Evie, this is getting out of control. I really think if you both just sat down and talked it out—"

"Okay, sure," I said quickly. "When?"

"How about today at lunch?"

"Great." Then I realized. "Oh, no. I *can't* today at lunch."

"Why not?"

"I have to . . . do something. Isn't there another time?"

Lily blinked. "I'll ask," she said. She got up and walked back over to Nisha, who gave her a look like, *See? What did I tell you!* And then Lily sat down next to her and started whispering and didn't come back.

So that, apparently, was that. If I couldn't meet Nisha at lunch today, then too bad for me.

I felt stunned, like someone had punched me in the stomach.

Because suddenly it was obvious that my best friends were giving up on me, like no matter what I said, they'd already made up their minds. And the truth was, I really *wanted* to sit down and talk, maybe not about Espee's love life, but about everything else. Except why did this talk have to be *today at lunch, Evie, take it or leave it*? How come Nisha always got to do all the organizing? It was hard to decide which was more unfair: the fact that they'd decided against me, or the fact that they were making all the rules, scheduling a talk with basically zero input from me.

I spent the rest of class jabbing brown paint on my sundae and listening to people gossiping about Kayla: how she broke it off with Zane, how upset she was, how mean he was, how she swears she's never dating anyone until college. Every once in a while I peeked over at Nisha and Lily, but mostly I tried to keep my eyes on Theo, who seemed strangely relaxed, wandering around the studio, helping people with their projects. Acting like, *Private life? What private life? I'm just a normal teacher doing my normal job.*

As soon as the bell rang, Francesca ran up to my side. "No visit from Espee," she murmured. "Guess she's waiting for lunch."

"Lunge," I corrected her, and she exploded in laughter. Then I shushed her right away because I realized Nisha was staring at us with a funny look on her face. And even though I was still upset about the lunch-or-never invitation, I didn't want things with Nisha to get any weirder.

Lunch was right after Music. The second the bell rang, Francesca and I ran to the cafeteria to grab two bags of Sun Chips, then sneaked back upstairs to Spush. Espee's door was closed, but there was light coming from underneath, and we could hear the random faraway sounds of that New Agey music she liked so much.

Maybe three minutes passed. Some kids walked by and stared at us, and so did the custodian, but we didn't move or talk or pretty much even breathe.

Finally we heard her voice: "Oh yes, but do you understand how strongly I feel?"

"Yee-haw," Francesca murmured. "It's happening, Evie!"

"Omigod," I whispered. "But are you sure he's in there? It could be—"

"Shh. Just listen!"

Then all of a sudden I had a terrible thought. I pointed frantically at Francesca's stilettos. "Take them off!" I mouthed.

She frowned. "Why? What's wrong—?"

"Noisy," I mouthed. I mimed running for dear life.

Francesca slapped her forehead, slipped off her shoes, and tucked them under one arm. "Eek," she whispered, smiling apologetically.

We waited again, my heart nearly bursting though the pumpkin sweater.

All of a sudden there were sounds near the door.

"I'm with you completely," said Theo's voice. "But don't you think maybe we should take a deep breath here?"

"No," Espee replied. "I'm sorry, Theo, but it's too late for that."

Francesca grinned ecstatically and gave me two giant thumbs-up.

Then we heard a shuffling sound. Shuffling like maybe feet.

I yanked Francesca's arm. "THEY'RE COMING," I mouthed. "LET'S *GO*."

We raced down the hallway, Francesca sliding in her knecsocks.

chapter 15

n Wednesday morning I bolted out of bed, took three bites of bagel, kissed Mom's cheek ("Evie?" she said suspiciously. "Everything okay?"), then raced across the yard to Samantha's house. All I could focus on was Theo and Espee; I didn't want to think about anything else.

Francesca was standing on the front steps in her zebra jacket. But she didn't grin or wave or even seem happy to see me. She just immediately handed me a big pink envelope. "Open it," she muttered.

So I did. It was a card with a picture of a smiling family sitting in front of a big blazing fireplace, all cuddled up with their dog and their cat. Over their heads was a quilt that read: A FAMILY IS FOREVER.

"Doesn't that just make you absolutely retch?" Francesca demanded. "Oh, wait, it gets worse. Read it."

Inside was a note in perfect mom-handwriting:

Dear Frankie, Just wanted to say one more time how sorry I am about that silly argument at the beach house last weekend. We hope to see you back there soon—and at our house ANY TIME. There's always a bed for you here— DON'T FORGET. All my love, Aunt Bitsy.

At the bottom of the page was another note written in a messy, slanty print:

P.S. Hey, Frankie, ask Evie for her screen name so I can IM her, OK? Tell her mine is scalawag. See you, Quentin.

I gave her back the card. "What's this not-forgetting business?" I asked, as we started walking to school.

"Ugh," said Francesca grumpily. "It's all so bloody boring.

Aunt Bitsy keeps begging me to come live with her. "

"She does? Why?"

"Who knows. She thinks Samantha isn't up to the job, or something."

I glanced at her. "But it's your choice, right?"

She sighed. "Well, I suppose *technically* it's my parents' choice. But they can't agree about bloody *anything*. Mother Darling wants me in Paris, but Daddy insists I'm better off with the aunts. And now the aunts are fighting; I hear Aunt Sam screaming on the phone every night." Suddenly her face brightened. "Oh, but what about that cute P.S.? Quentin wants your screen name. He likes you, Evie!"

"And I like him," I said truthfully. "But . . . well, I *really* like Zane." As soon as I said that, I realized I was blushing.

She put her arm around my shoulder. "So you finally admit your crush?"

"Yeah," I said, laughing now. "I guess I do."

"That's brilliant. Good for you, Evie! Well, don't worry about Quentin, I'll let him down easy. Now forget about my boring family and let's plan *all* about Theo and Espee!"

For a few minutes before Homeroom that morning, we hung out at the faculty mailroom, hoping to lip-read another rendezvous between Theo and Espee. But they didn't show up. Then we noticed that both their mailboxes were empty, so we thought maybe they'd just arrived early in the morning, for a romantic coffee. In Art we heard Theo tell Katie Finberg that she couldn't stop by at lunch to finish her papier-mâché project. He was "having a meeting with the principal," he said.

"Oh, sure," Francesca murmured, winking at me. "The *principal*."

So at lunch we snuck back upstairs to Espee's classroom. But this time her door was wide open, and we could hear Brendan Meyers's whiny voice inside. "I'll never finish this project! There's just too much stuff to read!" he was complaining.

"Yes, the Civil War is a very rich topic," she was answering sympathetically. "Have you seen this book? It's a little controversial, but—"

"Blah," Francesca muttered. "What a bore. Let's get out of here, Evie."

Spush wasn't any better. Espee gave us a surprise quiz about the Continental Congress, and then handed back some homework. Just like Theo, she seemed the same as always—maybe a bit less twinkly than usual, but today wasn't a twinkly sort of class, anyway.

When the period was over, Francesca leaned over my desk. "Well, so far today's been a bloody waste of time, don't you think? Let's give them one more chance."

"How? School's practically over," I whispered. Out of the corner of my eye I could see that Nisha and Lily looked upset, probably because I was whispering right in front of them. So I gave them both a really nice smile, but they just frowned and turned away. It felt like a cheek-slap, and I could feel my face reddening.

Now Francesca cupped her hand over my ear. "Meet me in the parking lot at dismissal. Maybe they'll leave together. Or maybe we'll witness a passionate farewell."

I nodded my answer so that at least I wouldn't be whispering.

The very second school was over, I ran out to the faculty parking lot, where Francesca waved me over to a giant Chevy Suburban. It was so huge that it made perfect cover, so we crouched behind it, peeking out as teachers slowly left the building and got into their cars. We were like that for almost fifteen minutes, and my knees were starting to cramp. I was just about to get up and stretch when Francesca hissed, "Don't move, Evie, it's *them*."

Theo and Espee were walking out of the building,

definitely together, definitely having some sort of intense conversation. Suddenly they stopped walking and faced each other, still talking, Theo's arms folded across his chest and Espee cocking her head to one side, exactly the way she did in Spush.

He said something that made him hold out his hands like he was asking, *What do you want from me?*

She stared at him. "You're saying we do *nothing*? I can't believe I'm hearing this!"

Francesca squeezed my elbow so hard, I almost screamed.

Theo said something quiet.

"No," Espee answered, her voice rising. "It's not that simple, Theo."

He said something else. She frowned and shook her head.

Then he looked at his watch. "All right," we heard him say. "Gotta go now. See you tomorrow, Steph."

We saw him get into his Explorer. Then Espee got into her Prius, and the two of them drove out of the parking lot in completely opposite directions.

"Well," Francesca said. She stood up and started dusting off her zebra jacket.

I got up slowly. "That didn't look too good, did it?"

"It looked *disastrous*," Francesca corrected me. "'You're saying we do nothing? It's not that simple.' How could he treat her that way? What an utter rejection."

"I also didn't like how his arms were folded," I said, strapping on my backpack. "And how he held out his hands. And how he looked at his watch."

Francesca picked up the cardboard folder she used for cramming in loose papers. "Right. You're totally right. His body language was hopeless."

"So was hers, actually. She looked like she was scolding a student."

"Exactly." Francesca sighed loudly. "I hate to say this, Evie, but the love letter was a failure. Because look what just happened: she bares her soul to him, she expresses her *truest feelings*, and he tells her they do nothing. *Nothing!* And then he drives off in his ugly SUV, like it never even happened. Oh, poor, poor Espee. She must feel absolutely devastated."

Like an empty, smashed-up soda can, I thought.

We trudged out of the parking lot, both of us feeling so sorry for Espee that we could barely talk.

couple of blocks later, Francesca suggested we go to I Scream "as a gesture of support to Espee," who, she said, was probably rushing right home to snarf down an entire pint of ice cream. I didn't argue; after what we'd just seen, the last thing I felt like doing was sitting at my computer and Googling the San Francisco Earthquake. Besides, I told myself, we owed something to Espee—maybe not sympathy–ice cream, but something real, something that would rescue her from Theo's cruel rejection. I had no idea what it could be, but I wanted to go somewhere and think seriously about the situation. So I said yes to Francesca's suggestion, even though I realized I'd probably be paying.

I Scream was crazy that afternoon, with a Cub Scout troop and a little kids' birthday party spilling out of the back room. As soon as Francesca and I walked in the door, we dumped our school stuff on a corner table and ordered two large chocolate shakes from Zane's dad. We'd just sat down with our shakes when Francesca announced that she desperately needed to go to the bathroom. "Don't steal my shake," she scolded, wagging her finger at me. "I'll be able to tell."

"Shut up," I answered, sticking out my tongue at her.

For a few minutes I sat there giving myself chocolate brain-freeze and watching this sweaty magician-type blowing up balloon dachshunds for the screaming birthday kids. And then, all of a sudden, Zane appeared out of the back room. He was wearing an I SCREAM FOR ICE CREAM T-shirt and a Bob the Builder party hat. And for some reason, he walked over and sat down in the empty chair next to me, that boy way, with his legs spread far apart.

"Evie," he said. "I was looking for you."

"You were?" I wiped my chocolate mustache with the back of my hand.

"About Friday." He blinked his beautiful gold-hazel eyes. "What about a movie?"

"What about one?" I said. And then it hit me. He was asking me *to* a movie.

HE WAS ASKING ME TO A MOVIE.

"Oh. Yeah, great," I said casually. "That sounds . . . great."

"We'll talk," he said, doing that head-jerk thing with his bangs. And then he got up from the table and walked back to the birthday room.

I nearly peed.

"Evie, are you okay?" Francesca asked like one-majillionth of a second later.

"Omigod," I answered. I stared at her.

"Did something just happen?"

"YES," I said. "Zane asked me out. To a MOVIE."

"That's wonderful!" She beamed at me. "It's what you wanted, right?"

I nodded. "But, I mean. It's *unbelievable*, Francesca. He barely even *spoke* to me before."

Francesca sat down and took a long sip of milk shake. "Well, you should have a little more self-confidence, Evie. You're a truly good person, you're smart, you're pretty, and my cousin liked you, so why shouldn't Zane?"

"Your cousin?"

"Quentin, remember? The cute P.S. on that hideous card? So what do you think you'll wear on Friday?"

"Wear?"

She laughed. "You'll need an outfit. Want to borrow something from Aunt Sam?"

"NO," I said, suddenly waking up. "I mean, no thanks! I'll just dress normally. I mean, normal for *me*."

"Well, what about those earrings?"

"You mean those gold dangly ones?"

"Just think about it, okay? You'll want to look gorgeous for your date."

"Yeah," I said, grinning like an idiot. "I'll think about it, Francesca."

Then I floated home.

Grace was sitting at the kitchen table doing her AP Bio. "Hey, Evie," she said as soon as I came in the door. "Are you okay? You look weird."

"I'm absolutely perfect." I sat down next to her. "Can I tell you something amazing?"

"If it's quick."

"Somebody asked me out."

She stared at me. "You mean like *on a date*?"

I nodded.

"Whoa. Well, you're not going, are you?"

"Sure I am. Why shouldn't I?"

"Because you're *in seventh grade*." She frowned at me. "Does Mom know about this?"

"How could she? I just got home!"

"Well, you'd better tell her tonight. And you should realize she'll probably say no."

My heart was starting to bang. "Why should she? It's just to the movies!"

"Evie, *I* never went out when *I* was in seventh grade."

"Well, what does that have to do with me? You're you, and I'm—"

"Too immature to be dating."

"How would you know?" I could feel my armpits getting wet. "Besides, tons of people date in seventh grade!"

"Well, maybe that's because they have messed-up priorities."

"*What?*"

"Maybe they aren't putting academics first. The way they should be, at your age."

"So according to you," I said in a loud ha-ha sort of voice, "unless I freak out the way *you* did in seventh grade,

I'm totally messed up? Is that what you're saying?"

Grace looked slapped. "I didn't *freak out,* I *focused.* Unlike you, apparently."

"What? I'm completely focused!"

"On what?"

"Lots of things." I didn't want to say "Theo and Espee," so I added, "School. And also having a life."

"Let me tell you something," Grace said. "You can focus on *school,* or you can focus on *having a life.* You can't focus on both." Then she shut her book and stomped out of the kitchen.

Well, what does Grace know? I thought. *Why CAN'T I have both?* I remembered what Francesca had told me that night on the beach: "School is not the whole wide world." Plenty of things were just as important—love, for example. Of course Grace wouldn't understand this, because all she cared about was schoolwork. In fact, that was all my whole family seemed to care about—work, work, work. I suddenly felt sorry for them—sorry for everyone but Francesca, who actually asked herself cosmos questions and thought about things like *soulmates.* Even Espee understood that life was bigger than Blanton Middle School. If only she could be as blissfully happy as I was right now.

❂

It turned out that Mom had an endless real estate dinner that night, so I couldn't talk to her about the date business until the morning. Which was fine with me, actually. Because as long as she hadn't said I couldn't go, I could imagine Friday night any way I liked: me with earrings, me without earrings. That night I went to bed so ecstatic, I thought I might even wear my amber necklace to school tomorrow. After all, Nisha wasn't talking to me, so she couldn't tease me about the prehistoric mosquito. And since Zane *had asked me out*, it was okay to wear a (sort of) love token. Although maybe, I thought, it would be better to save it for Friday, in honor of my first-ever date.

I lay in bed for a long time wishing there were stars outside my window. And thinking: *Necklace. Boyfriend. Love token.*

Okay, not love token. But close enough.

And that was when I had the best, most incredible idea ever. Of my entire life.

chapter 17

It turned out Grace was right about one thing: Mom *did* have a have a problem with the whole Dating in Seventh Grade thing. But at breakfast on Thursday morning she said it would be okay with her if the movie was a "group outing." Which meant that I could go if, like, fifteen people joined us, and we all wore identical T-shirts and went to the bathroom buddy-system. Okay, I'm exaggerating. But the bottom line was, as long as we invited a bunch more kids, I could have my movie date with Zane. So at 7:30, when I went to ring Francesca's doorbell, I was still basically delirious.

Plus, I had spent the night thinking about My Incredible

Idea, which I sprang on Francesca the second she opened the door.

"Remember that locket your aunt's boyfriend gave her? The one she doesn't wear anymore?"

"Evie? What are you babbling about?" Francesca scowled at me in the sunlight, as if she'd just woken up thirty seconds ago. And she probably had: Her eyes were squinty, her hair was a snarled mess, and she was drinking something out of a stainless-steel commuter cup.

"The silver locket," I reminded her. "With the fancy initials. It was in the box called 'Vintage.' You showed it to me, remember?"

"God, it's too early in the day to remember anything. Come inside," she grunted, and took a big sip from her cup. "You want some Mochaccino?"

A rabbit scampered across her feet, but she didn't even notice.

"Listen to me, Francesca," I said, the words just rushing out of my mouth. "You know how the letter didn't work, how humiliated Espee felt in the parking lot yesterday? Well, she'll never get anywhere with Theo if she just gives up! But what if she thought he loved her back? Don't you think her body language would be different? And maybe even her clothes? And don't you think Theo would look at her like, I don't know what, but definitely *not like a teacher*?"

Francesca raised one eyebrow. "Go on."

"So I've been thinking: What could convince Espee of Theo's love? She's feeling incredibly insecure right now, so it would have to be something specific. But also beautiful, because he's an artist, right? And then I remembered that heart-shaped locket. I mean, I know she never wears jewelry, but I bet she would if she thought it was a love token. Because 'SP, TR.' How could it *not* be from Theo?"

"Tristan Royce, Theo Rafferty," Francesca murmured. "Samantha Pattison, Stephanie Pierce."

I grinned. "The very same initials. Isn't it such an amazing coincidence, Francesca? Don't you think it totally feels like fate?"

"Yes, it does," she said slowly. "Un-cruel fate. So what are you saying? We should plant Samantha's locket on her desk? Or maybe stick it in her mailbox?"

"Her desk is better." As soon as I said that, I could feel my heart start to race. "I've been thinking about this all night. The faculty mailroom is too public. Somebody might see us."

"Evie Webber," Francesca said. She stared for about

three more seconds, then threw her arms around me. "YOU are an UTTER GENIUS. Did you know that about yourself? Did you realize that you were an utter, utter—"

"Ack. You're squeezing me."

"Sorry. You're ridiculously skin and bones. And an UTTER GENIUS. What an ABSOLUTELY BRILLIANT IDEA. It's gorgeous. No, it's better than gorgeous. It's . . . STAGGERINGLY EPIC."

"Shh," I said, beaming. "You'll wake up Samantha."

"She's already up. Big audition this morning." Her eyes widened. "Perfect timing, come to think of it. We can sneak upstairs and get the locket while she's in the shower."

"You mean now?"

"No time like the present." She took one last gulp of Mochaccino and then we tiptoed quickly up the stairs. Without Francesca reminding me, I slipped off my shoes outside Samantha's bedroom. Then we tiptoed inside.

"*Don't cry for me, Argentina,*" Samantha was singing in her shower. "*You were sup-posed to be immortal . . .*"

"You stay here," Francesca whispered. "I'll get the locket."

I suddenly remembered that the boxes were in the closet room on the other side of the bathroom. Francesca would have to sneak past her singing aunt *both ways*. "Wait! Won't she see you?"

"Not through the steam," she replied. And immediately I knew she'd done this before.

I stood barefoot in the fabulous boudoir listening to Samantha belt out show tunes, and also to the chandelier: *plinka plinka plinka*, the most beautiful faraway music. Only it wasn't faraway, it was right here. And so was I. The weird thing was, I felt like I belonged. Even though of course I was totally trespassing.

"Got it," Francesca mumbled as she burst out of the bathroom. "Now let's get out of here. Fast!"

I grabbed my shoes and my backpack, and we ran out the door and all the way to Blanton Middle School, laughing like crazy.

Once we got to school, the big question was: How could we get the locket onto Espee's desk without her—or anyone else, for that matter—noticing? Francesca had a fantastic plan: One of us would distract her, and the other one would slip inside the classroom and plant the locket on her desk.

"But since the whole thing is your idea, you get dibs," she said, which I thought was incredibly generous.

I told her I wanted to plant the locket.

"Lovely," Francesca said. "All right, Evie, let's think. She usually gets a container of yogurt for lunch, right? So on her way upstairs from the lunchroom I'll stop her to talk about U.S. History, and you'll break into Spush."

"Break in? Not *break in*, Francesca!"

"Go in. Walk in. Whatever you want to call it."

"*Walk in* is fine." I considered the plan for a second. "Wait, wait! You'll stop her to talk about *U.S. History*? Won't that seem a little, uh, suspicious?"

"I'll ask her about the San Francisco Earthquake, okay? Don't worry about *me*. Everything is going to be absolutely perfect!"

Then Francesca handed me the locket, which I quickly rolled up in a tissue and stuffed into my pants pocket.

It all went according to plan. Francesca was a chatty talker, which meant I had plenty of time to position the locket perfectly on Espee's overflowing desk. I have to admit that just being alone in Espee's classroom was as big a thrill as standing all alone in Samantha's boudoir—in a way, an even bigger thrill, because I knew I was doing something wonderful and important for someone who desperately needed my help. So I made the moment last as long as I could, listening to the classroom clock tick, and also to the busy humming sound of Espee's computer.

Then I ran downstairs to the lunchroom, where Francesca was standing by the frozen yogurt machine, squirting herself a gigantic bowlful.

As soon as she saw me she put down her bowl. "How did it go?"

"It went," I said.

We fist-bumped and grinned at each other.

"I'm so fantastically proud of you, Evie," Francesca murmured, her green eyes shining. "You're utterly transformed; you're the opposite of paralyzed."

"You think so?"

"Oh, it's obvious. You're like a whole new Evie Webber."

A whole new Evie Webber. I actually felt goosebumps. Not the cold kind or the nervous kind. The incredibly happy-and-excited kind.

Then Francesca picked up her cardboard bowl and took an enormous spoonful of frozen yogurt. "And now," she said, swallowing it all in one gulp, "we sit back, twiddle our thumbs, and wait to see what happens."

chapter 18

We didn't have to wait long.

As we were walking down the hall to Spush, we could see Espee standing in front of the classroom chatting with Kayla and Gaby, who was doing her car-alarm laugh. I couldn't imagine why. Was Espee making some kind of joke? It was hard to imagine her saying something that Gaby would find so hysterically funny. On the other hand, Gaby was the type to laugh at anything.

Finally the horrible laughing stopped. And we were maybe ten steps away from them when I noticed something shiny around Espee's neck.

It was the locket.

Tristan's present to Samantha.

Which Espee was *actually wearing*.

"Francesca," I said.

"Brilliant," she murmured. "Stay calm, Evie." Suddenly her voice sounded loud and cheerful. "Oh, hello, Ms. Pierce. Thanks for chatting with me before about the earthquake. Those books you recommended sound absolutely fantastic."

Espee blinked. Whatever she'd just said to Gaby, she looked totally serious now. "Really? Well, I'm glad I was so helpful."

"Oh, you were! I think I'll stop by the library this afternoon and try to find them."

I wanted to add something impressive-sounding about my own research, but I could feel my cheeks burning stupidly, and I thought that at any moment I might burst into nervous giggles. Plus, I could see that Kayla was rolling her eyes at Gaby. So I poked Francesca.

"All right, well, see you inside," she said brightly to Espee, and we walked into the room. As soon as we were inside, Francesca clapped her hands. "Yee-haw, it worked! She's wearing the locket, so that's Step One in the self-esteem makeover. Now we've got to get her out of those clothes and into something less tragic."

"How?" I said, laughing. "You're going to stuff one of Samantha's sarongs into her mailbox?"

Francesca laughed too. "Yes, yes, perfect! Oh, Evie, you're on fire! Do you think she likes tropical flowers?"

Of course all I could think about the entire Spush was planting the sarong—not in the mailbox, but somewhere private and discreet, like maybe in one of the cupboards in Espee's classroom, or in the small closet where she stored her maps. I wanted to spend the afternoon planning this out with Francesca, and also settling on which sarong we'd steal from Samantha's collection. But at dismissal Francesca told me she couldn't, because one of her aunts—I think she said it was Beebee—was coming over to Samantha's "just to check in."

"Check in on what?" I asked, not even trying to hide my disappointment.

"Who knows. The rabbits, probably. Anyway, it'll be a complete waste of *my* afternoon, but at least *you'll* have some time to work on your movie date. Have you thought who else to ask yet?"

"Not really." The truth was, I'd been so busy thinking

about Espee's love life, I hadn't been focusing on Friday night. "So far there's you, me, and Zane."

"Not enough to satisfy Mom, I presume. What about Nisha and Lily?"

I shrugged. "I told you, Francesca. Things are sort of weird."

Francesca frowned. "That utterly makes no sense. You should at least ask them if they'd *like* to go. It's your first date—you shouldn't exclude your best friends!"

"Yeah," I said, biting my lip. "Except maybe they're not anymore."

"Don't be deranged, Evie. Of course they are; you three have been best friends *forever*, right? And forever means forever, like that hideous card said. So just because you're friends with *me* now—"

"Whoa, stop," I interrupted. "This is not about you, okay?"

"It's not? I thought they had a problem with me."

"Yeah, maybe," I admitted. "But it's more like they had a problem with *me*."

"Why? What did you do?"

"I'm not even sure." I sighed. "I guess you could say I wouldn't obey their rules."

It was funny. Because when I said that, I guess I was expecting Francesca to say something like, *Oh, you hate rules too, now. You're just like me!*

But that's not what she said. She said, "Well, figure it out, Evie. *Talk* to them, ask them on your date, and also ask some b-o-y-s, please! Now I'd better go, or else Beebee will be furious." Then she blew me a kiss, buttoned her zebra jacket, and ran out of the building in Samantha's cowboy boots.

That day I walked home by myself, which was something I hadn't done in a long, long time. I thought about inviting Nisha and Lily—I really did—but I couldn't even remember the last time we'd had a real, no-fighting, face-to-face-to-face conversation. So I couldn't imagine calling them and being all, *Hey, what's up, and oh, by the way, ZANE ASKED ME OUT and would you like to come?* I could already hear Nisha's response: *Zane who? I thought you didn't even like him.* Or: *Oh, so now we're on speaking terms? Because your mom says you need some date-buddies?* Or: *Sorry, Evie, but Lily and I are working on our Attic Project. Have a nice night.* And of course Lily would be all sweet and sympathetic, but in the end she'd just go off with Nisha, the way she always did.

I needed to face reality: Things were bad with my best

friends. Really bad. Dangerously bad. And if I didn't fix it all soon, our friendship might be permanently wrecked. But inviting them on my Zane-date was not going to solve anything. In fact, even talking to them about it would probably just make things worse.

But if not them, who should I ask? I couldn't invite Kayla because . . . well, I was pretty sure you didn't invite ex-girlfriends along on a date. And if Kayla was out, that meant so was Gaby. I thought about Katie Finberg; she was a little bit perfect-perfect, but she was basically a decent person. And Brendan Meyers would probably be okay, as long as he wore deodorant and didn't spit. I told myself that five people (me, Zane, Francesca, Katie Finberg, and spitty Brendan) had to count as a big enough date for Mom. Because five was a definite group, right? Even without Nisha and Lily.

As soon as I got home I grabbed a glass of ice cubes and went upstairs to my computer. *No excuses,* I lectured myself: *You've focused on Espee for two days straight and you've just planned Friday night, so now you're going to sit down and do some serious earthquake research!* And I actually did spend about twenty minutes Googling tremors and aftershocks and the Richter scale.

But then somehow my brain just kind of wandered off. And before I realized exactly what I was doing, I was Googling *Zane Gerety*. All that came up was a dorky article in the *Blanton Register* about I Scream. But there was a super-cute photo of him behind the counter, which I stared at for a ridiculously long time.

Then I Googled *Stephanie Pierce*. Espee had signed a bunch of petitions for some candidate I'd never heard of. Also, according to the *Register*, she was the star pitcher on a women's softball team called the Blanton Bliss (I know, I know: dumb name). At the end of the article was a photo of her hugging a giant trophy, and grinning ear-to-ear, as if she were about eight years old. It was a very nice picture, I thought, even though I couldn't imagine that grinning person wearing a sarong. But today she wore Theo's locket, so who could tell what else she'd do, if she actually had the chance? And of course now she would have the chance, thanks to her two fairy godmothers. I grinned back at her, because it felt as if we shared a secret.

The last name I Googled was *Theo Rafferty*. Not surprisingly, I guess, Theo had his own artist's website, with lots of complicated pages to navigate: *New Works. Gallery Showings. Home Studio. Reviews*. I poked around for a bit, peeking at his giant, abstract canvases, which looked exactly like Mom's veggie stir-fries, if you want my honest opinion.

Then I noticed a link called *At Home with the Artist*. That looked a little more interesting, so I clicked on it.

And found myself staring at photos. Of Theo with his dog.

And Theo with his baby.

And Theo with his wife.

chapter 19

"E vie? What are you doing here?" Francesca asked, frowning. "I told you before, Aunt Beebee—"

"I know," I said through my teeth. "But this is a major emergency."

"What happened?"

"Where's your aunt?"

"In the living room. What does that—"

"He's married."

"Who is?"

"Who do you *think*? Theo!"

"He is? How do you even—"

"Frankie?" someone called from inside. "Is someone at the door?"

"Just Evie," she answered brightly. She yanked me inside to the living room, where Aunt Yellowteeth was sipping tea. "She came over about that project we're doing. Apparently it's hit a snag."

If I hadn't been totally freaking out right then, I'd have laughed. *Hit a snag?* Where did she even get these expressions?

"What a shame," Aunt Yellowteeth commented. "But you know, girls, that's life for you. One snag after another." She smiled at us, showing off her huge yellow teeth. Then she put down her teacup. "Well, I suppose this is my cue to shove off. Tell Sammy to ring me tonight, all right, Frankie dear?" She gave Francesca a quick hug, waved at me, and left.

"He's married?" Francesca asked as soon as the door clicked shut. "Are you sure?"

"Of course I'm sure! I read it on his website, like, three minutes ago."

She scrunched her forehead.. "Funny that he posts it on his website, but he doesn't even bother wearing a ring."

"Maybe he doesn't want to get papier-mâché all over it." I sank onto the sofa. "Omigod, what have I done?"

this is me from now on

"You haven't done anything, Evie."

"How can you say that? Espee thinks he's in love with her because of the locket, which was *my* stupid idea. This whole thing is all my stupid fault!"

Francesca sat down on the sofa and patted my knee. "Don't be so negative. Theo and Espee are just soulmates, like Cathy and Heathcliff. Sometimes people are just *meant* to be together."

"And no one else matters?" I demanded. "Theo has a life! A wife and a baby. And a dog named Ozzie!"

"Calm down. You're going a tad berserk. Anyway, true love is bigger than dogs named Ozzie."

"Oh, really? Really? Is that how you felt when your mom ran off to Paris?"

Francesca blinked. "What does that have to do with anything?"

"Did you feel like *her* true love was bigger than *your* family?"

Now her eyes blazed. "You have absolutely *no idea* what you're talking about." She shook her head and stared at the coffee-colored carpet. Then she looked right at me and said, "My mother is an extremely passionate person. She left Daddy because he didn't understand her."

❀ **193** ❀

"Oh. Well, sorry."

"Okay. But you shouldn't just *mention* her like that."

"I said I was sorry."

"Okay! Never mind."

We sat there for a minute not saying anything. Finally I took a long, wobbly breath. "Anyway, what I really mean is, we need to think about the whole picture here. We were planning on stealing a *sarong* for Espee, and Theo has a *family*. It's just wrong, Francesca. We have to break them up!"

"Evie, you know what your problem is?"

"I don't have a problem."

"Yes, you do: You haven't read *Wuthering Heights*. I truly do not understand how you can spend one more day without reading that book."

I stared at her. Was this girl deaf? Not-psychic-but-psychotic? "Francesca," I said, my voice coming out squawky, "this isn't Wuthering Heights, okay? This is Blanton. And we can't go around ruining someone's life just for fun. Ruining the lives of four people!"

"Four?"

I held up four fingers, like this was *Sesame Street*. "Espee, Theo. Wife, baby. And I'm leaving out the dog."

"Oh, of course," Francesca said distractedly. "Anyway, Evie, it wasn't for fun. It was only to *help* them."

I opened my mouth to argue, but before I could get a word out she said, "Well, sure. We'll break them up. If you absolutely insist."

"I do!"

"But how?" She scowled. Then her face lit up. "Wait, I have a fantastic idea. We could send Theo an ice cream cake with a message like, 'It's All Over, Boyfriend, Go Home to Ozzie.'"

"Are you serious?"

"You're right. Too many letters, and it would probably melt by the time we got to school. Well, we could always just send him another letter."

I snorted. "Quoting what? The Declaration of Independence?"

"Hmm, that's a little geeky, but coming from Espcc, it could possibly work."

"I was joking, Francesca. Not quoting anything."

"You mean just make something up?"

"NO!"

"Yeah, too risky. We'd probably misspell something, and then he'd know it wasn't from her. It was so much better just using what she wrote: 'O my darling, how I wish I could look into your eyes and express my truest—'"

"Gah. *Please* shut up."

"Sorry. But she's such a gorgeous writer, don't you think? Ooh, wait a sec—I just thought of something. Remember that hideous card Aunt Bitsy sent? 'A family is forever'? We could slip it in his mailbox, as a subtle reminder."

"That's completely stupid," I announced. "The picture is all wrong, and what about your aunt's note? And the P.S. from Quentin?"

"I'll rip off the front. It'll just be like a postcard, like the kind dentists send when they want to remind you to keep an appointment. Only this will remind Theo about, you know—"

"His family." I thought about it quickly. It was an incredibly dumb idea, maybe the worst one Francesca had ever had. But it wasn't as if I had a better one right then. And we had to do something, as fast as possible.

"We'll send the post card," I muttered. "Until we think of something else."

"Oh, we will, Evie," Francesca promised. "Don't worry about *that*."

chapter 20

n Friday we got to school early enough to sneak into the faculty mailroom before Theo had picked up his mail for the day. Francesca was in a great mood, as if overnight she'd convinced herself that breaking up Theo and Espee was just as *helpful* as getting them together. It didn't even matter to her that Topaz had nibbled the top right-hand corner of the card so that it now looked as if it said A FAMILY IS FOREV. "Don't worry, he'll think it's slang," Francesca whispered as she stuffed the chewed-up card-half into Theo's mailbox.

All morning long I had a giant knot in my stomach. In Art I couldn't even look at Theo. I just kept seeing him in all those smiling photos, and wondering how much longer everyone would be smiling. Finally, to distract myself, I painted a majillion rainbow sprinkles on my papier-mâché sundae and also forced myself to plan what I'd wear on my date that night.

Right before lunch I ran into Zane in the hall. I'd been dreading his reaction when I told him about needing a group-date, so I blurted it all out, just to get it over with.

"Whatever, Evie," he said, shrugging. "This was your thing, anyway."

Which I totally didn't understand. And which made me feel sort of weird, to tell you the truth.

But at least he didn't seem angry. And he didn't even seem to care who was going with us, which was a relief. I decided to take this as a sign to grab a taco and sit myself at a sticky table with Katie and Brendan.

"Hey," I said super-casually, like I did this all the time. "What are you guys doing tonight?"

"*This* night?" Brendan demanded. "You're talking about *today*?"

Brendan had a way of being specific and making sure everyone else was too. There was no point fighting him about it, so I just nodded.

"What's so special about tonight?" he asked suspiciously.

"Nothing," I said. "I'm just going to a movie and I wondered if you wanted to come. Both you guys." I smiled hopefully at Katie.

She smiled back with major braces. "Which movie?"

"I'm not sure yet."

Brendan grunted. "You're asking us to a movie but you don't even know which *one*?"

"It's not just up to me," I said, feeling my cheeks start to burn. "Zane is going too."

"He is?" Katie squealed. "Is this like a date? Between you and Zane?"

"Please keep it down," I begged. I could see that Nisha and Lily were sitting two tables away, and their backs were very straight, as if they were paying close attention to something. This conversation, probably. Well, it wasn't like I meant to keep it a secret from them. And to be honest, I had a giant urge right then to run over to their table and just invite them along. But of course that was impossible. Totally impossible.

"Whoa, that's awesome, Evie!" Katie was exclaiming. "Remember how bad you felt when Zane was going out with Kayla?"

Brendan scowled. "Is this going to be girl-talk now? Because if it is—"

"Sorry," I said quickly. "So, anyway, can you both come?"

"I can!" Katie said, grinning at me.

"I *guess* I can," Brendan admitted. "I mean, even if the movie sucks, it's better than spending Friday night working on that stupid Attic Project."

Katie pretend-punched his arm. "Brendan hates our project, but I think it's sort of cool. And romantic."

"Really?" I said, nibbling the cheese off my taco.

"Oh, definitely. We're doing a Mystery Box from the Civil War. There's this soldier and his fiancée writing letters back and forth, and he's describing the battlefields and she's talking about the homefront."

"And also her undying love," Brendan added. He put his hand on his heart and said in a cartoony, high-pitched voice, 'O my darling, how I wish I could look into your eyes . . .'"

My heart bounced. "What?"

". . . and express my truest feelings. But cruel fate has come between us—"

"That was in your Mystery Box? 'O my darling, how I wish—?'"

"Why?" Brendan asked. "Is it from something?"

I shook my head. *Omigod,* I screamed at myself. *Espee's computer! It wasn't a love letter to Theo Rafferty. It was just a pseudo-document for the Attic Project! Which I completely misinterpreted. And which Francesca—*

"Okay, see you guys at the theater," I mumbled. "Be there at seven." Then I raced over to the frozen yogurt machine, where Francesca was fixing herself another giant bowlful of vanilla.

"Come with me," I hissed at her. "Emergency."

She put down her cardboard bowl and followed me into the hall. "What's wrong now?"

I repeated what I'd just heard. Word for word.

Francesca blinked. "So Espee's writing was a fake? Well, that's . . . funny."

"You think it's *funny*? It's a *disaster.*"

She patted my arm. "Deep breaths, Evie. How were you supposed to know Espee was writing fake history? And the letter we mailed didn't even work, right? Remember how they acted afterward, in the parking lot? It was your genius locket idea that did the trick. Besides, we're breaking them up now, aren't we?"

I stood there shaking my head. Was she only pretending not to get it? Could she really not understand how awful this was?

Because what if we couldn't break them up? What if it was too late?

What if the whole romance—beginning with the gorgeous words on Espee's computer—was caused by my terrible, stupid, gigantic mistake?

Right before Spush, Nisha and Lily walked over to my locker, where I was throwing random books into my backpack.

"Okay, Evie, you want to talk about this?" Nisha asked.

Yes. Desperately. "I can't."

"Why not?"

Because you'd just say everything was my own fault. And you'd be right.

"Things are slightly complicated," I mumbled.

"And you also can't talk about your date with Zane?"

"We heard you in the lunchroom," Lily said quietly. "So did everyone else."

"I'm sorry," I said stupidly. "I wanted to tell you guys—"

"But you were too busy sneaking around with Francesca," Nisha said. Her eyes didn't look angry. They looked disappointed. Hurt. "Evie, *why*?"

"Please don't ask," I begged. "It's just this . . . project we were doing."

"The Attic Project?" Lily asked.

"No, a different one."

"Who's it for?"

"I can't tell you." The words came out of me like a sob. "I really want to, you can't *believe* how much I want to. But please just let me get through this, okay?"

Lily glanced at Nisha, who shrugged in disgust.

"Whatever," Nisha said finally. "You know what, Evie? It doesn't even matter anymore."

Then my two best friends turned and walked away.

chapter 21

The whole rest of that day, I just kept thinking *Zane, Zane, Zane.* It was the only way I could deal with worrying about Theo and Espee, wondering if he'd even read the chewed-up card, or just tossed it in the trash like a piece of junk mail. But I did spot them huddling in front of the main office right before dismissal, and I heard her whisper-yell at him, "Don't tell me how I'm supposed to feel about this!"—which *might* have meant he'd confessed about Ozzie and she was totally freaking out. The other thing I noticed was that Espee wasn't wearing the locket— although for all I knew she had it hidden under her lumpy white turtleneck sweater.

And of course their love affair wasn't the only thing in my life that was weird or complicated or just incredibly messed up. As of Spush, Nisha and Lily had completely stopped talking to me, and the fact that I had no idea how to fix things with them was really starting to terrify me. Plus I suddenly realized that Angelica's diary hadn't arrived this week, which meant that unless it showed up in the mail today, we were seriously running out of time. But I knew there was no point nagging Francesca about it, because apparently Samantha and Aunt Yellowteeth had a big screaming argument on the phone last night, and Francesca announced that she "absolutely refused to discuss" her "utterly boring family."

Anyway, with all this chaos going on, the one thing that was totally good, the one thing that made me feel happy and un-paralyzed, was thinking about my movie date with Zane. Even Francesca seemed eager to help me obsess. We hung out together that afternoon, me sort of research-ing the San Francisco Earthquake online while she pulled books off my shelves and asked tons of random questions: Was I planning to wear the Oscar earrings? Did I know anything about the movie? Would we go to I Scream after-ward? Did I want to borrow shoes?

barbara dee

We also spent a lot of time in my bathroom, doing and redoing my hair. Finally we decided how it should look (pretty much the same as always, although parted a little farther to the left). I showed her the outfit I was planning to wear (purple top with cute embroidery, blue mini with cute pockets, black ballet flats). Then she asked, for the majillionth time, about the Oscar earrings.

"Actually," I admitted, "I think I've decided to wear this instead." I opened my desk drawer and took out my amber necklace. "That's a prehistoric mosquito," I explained quickly, before she could even ask.

She held up the necklace to my desk lamp. "My God."

"I bought it with my own money. This summer at the mall. Don't say you hate it."

"Why would I?"

"I don't know. Because of the mosquito."

"The mosquito," she said, "is absolutely brilliant. The mosquito gives it *character*." She clutched her chest like she was having a heart attack. "Oh, Evie. This necklace is deeply, deeply gorgeous."

"It is?"

"It's epic. It's fantastic. It's utterly unique."

"You really—?"

"It's you," she said, giving me her dazzling smile.

And that was when I forgave her for everything. Because how could you stay even a tiny bit mad at someone who gets who you really are? Or who you would be if you weren't afraid? She handed the necklace back to me, and then I fastened it around my neck. And I thought: *This is me from now on.* I'm not even sure what I meant by that. But once it was on, I promised myself that I'd never take it off. No matter what anyone else ever said about it.

Around six Francesca went home to feed the rabbits and, I supposed, to get dressed. Mom was doing an open house for this big, ugly McMansion she was selling, so Grace ordered in some Chinese food. (She was still acting huffy about my date, so all she got was spicy shrimp, which she knew I hated. But that was okay, because I was too excited to eat, anyway.)

The second Dad got home from work, I gave him an enormous hug. "You didn't forget, right? You're driving Francesca and me to the Blanton Cineplex at exactly 6:55, right?"

"Right," he said, tiredly. "Just let me put my briefcase down first, okay, Evie?"

Francesca rang the bell at 6:50 wearing her huge cable-knit sweater and some normal-looking jeans. Her hair was in a messy ponytail, and for once she was wearing actual sneakers. "You look fabulous," she shouted as soon as I opened the door.

"Thanks. So do you," I said, wondering why she'd changed her clothes into something so . . . un-Francesca. But I didn't wonder too hard, because after all, this wasn't her date. So who cared what she looked like, anyway?

We got to the movie theater at 6:57. Katie Finberg was reading a paperback, and Brendan Meyers was talking on his cell phone and pacing in front of the ticket window.

"Which one's Zane?" Dad asked, as he pulled over. "The one on the phone?"

"Lord NO," Francesca exclaimed. "That's Hideous Brendan. His personal habits are disgusting, truthfully."

Dad glared at the honking car behind us. "Well, I'll meet Zane later, I guess. Got your cell, Evie?"

"Yup!"

"Call me by nine fifteen."

"So early? The movie's over at nine ten!"

"I know. Call and we'll talk. Have fun."

"Oh, we will, Mr. Webber!" Francesca promised. "Thanks extremely for the lift!"

And then we were on the sidewalk.

Immediately Brendan paced over to us. "Where's Zane? Wasn't he coming with you?"

I shook my head.

"Why not? You guys are supposed to be on a date, right?"

I nodded.

"Well, I checked the times, and the movie's starting in, like, six minutes." Saying the words "six minutes" sprayed some spit on his upper lip. It was so gross, I had to look down at my shoes.

"I'm sure Zane is on his way," Francesca said quickly.

I looked up. She had a funny expression on her face, one I'd never seen before, kind of like a battle between *Isn't this funfunfun* and *Omigod, this could be a bloody disaster.*

"Well, anyway, I'll get in line to buy our tickets," she announced loudly. "And if Zane is running a tad late, we'll just save him a seat."

Everyone handed her some money. I grabbed her sweater. "What if he isn't coming?" I whispered.

"He's absolutely coming," she whispered back. "He told me."

"He did? When?"

"I don't know, the other day. Don't worry, Evie. Just enjoy your date."

"Does anyone else want popcorn?" Katie asked. "I can't watch a movie if I don't have buttered popcorn."

"Except the stuff they use isn't butter," Brendan said. "Just Buttery-Flavored Oil."

"Eww, gross," Katie squealed. "Don't ruin it for me, Brendan!"

He grinned. "Actually, as long as you're getting popcorn can you get me some nachos? With Cheese-Flavored Product?"

"Normal people call it *cheese*," Katie reminded him. "Evie, do you want anything?"

I suddenly had an intense craving for an extra-large cup of crushed ice. And I definitely didn't want to be left alone with Brendan. So I followed Katie over to the concession stand.

We watched the concession guy drown her popcorn in Buttery-Flavored Oil. As soon as he was done, Katie took one soggy-looking kernel between her thumb and pointer and popped it daintily into her mouth. Then she wiped her mouth with a napkin and said, "Can I ask you a question, Evie? Are you still fighting with Nisha and Lily?"

I scooped some ice into a paper cup. "Why do you ask?"

"Because it's funny they're not here."

I tried to spot Francesca on the ticket line, but the lobby was getting too crowded to see anything. "Oh, that's because they're working on their Attic Project."

"Too bad," Katie said like she probably didn't believe me. She reached for Brendan's nachos. "So how's your project going, anyway?"

"Mine? Oh. Really, really well."

"What's it on?"

"It's . . . hard to describe." I checked my watch: 7:04. "Because it's family history. And families get, you know, sort of . . . complicated. How's yours?"

"Great. Brendan complains a lot, but he's actually a great partner. We're just working on the bibliography, and then we're pretty much done."

"Cool," I said, chomping hard on my ice. And thinking: *If only I'd partnered with Katie Finberg. Not only would I be pretty much done with the Attic Project but I wouldn't be ruining the lives of four people.*

Plus a dog.

A minute later Francesca returned with five adult tickets.

It was now exactly one minute until they started showing the previews, so I told everyone to get seats, while I waited in the lobby for Zane. Francesca offered to hang out with me, but I said there was no point in both of us missing the start of the movie. ("Are you absolutely sure?" she asked, the *omigod* side winning the battle on her face. "I totally am," I answered firmly, chewing on the last little molecules of ice in my cup.) So she went into the theater with the others and I sat there by myself, watching car-crash trailers over and over on the overhead TV sets and tracing rectangles with my shoe in the geometric carpeting.

At 7:32, Zane strolled into the lobby.

"Hey," he said casually. "Sorry I'm late. Where's everybody else?"

"Inside," I said, handing him a ticket. "Is everything okay?"

"Why wouldn't it be?"

We hurried into the dark theater. Brendan and Katie were sitting at the end of a row, and Francesca was sitting behind them, next to two seats on the aisle. Zane immediately took the empty seat right next to her, leaving me on the end. I saw him lean over and whisper something in her ear, and then I saw her whisper something back. It sounded like *You promised*. Promised what? To be on time? Not to whisper during the movie? He whispered something again, then folded his arms across his chest.

Francesca leaned across Zane and beamed at me. "So, Evie," she said. "Isn't this great?"

"Great," Zane muttered.

"You be quiet. I think everything is *perfect*."

"Yeah, Francesca. If you say so."

He slumped low in his seat like his whole body was pouting, and suddenly I understood something I should have seen right from the beginning. How could I have been so blind? About so many different things? It was as if for the past two weeks my brain had been stuck on Pause, and now I was fumbling in the dark for the Play button.

Francesca tapped on the back of Katie's seat. "Could I possibly have a tiny bit of popcorn?" she asked sweetly. "That butter smell is heaven."

"Oh, sure," Katie said. She turned around, holding up her greasy tub. "You guys want some also?" she asked, a smear under her lip, like a buttery-flavored soul patch.

"No thanks," Zane grumbled. "I just want to see the movie."

"Evie?"

"No thanks."

Francesca reached into the tub and took a giant handful. "Ooh, lovely," she said. "Really salty and greasy. I bet those nachos are yummy too."

So now Brendan turned around. "You want one?" he asked, even though you could tell he didn't want to share.

Francesca helped herself to a big gooey orange glob. "Bliss," she exclaimed, as if she wasn't even in a movie theater. "Of course now I'm thirsty."

That did it for me. I reached inside my jean jacket and pulled out a five-dollar bill. Then I leaned across Zane and handed it to her. "If you want something, go get your own," I whispered loudly.

Then I sat there watching the movie. It was about some guy who saved the world, but I didn't even notice what from.

chapter 22

ren't you going to answer the phone?" Grace said at breakfast Saturday morning.

I shook my head. Now that she knew my First-Ever Date had been a humiliating disaster, and that I never wanted to go on another one for, like, *the entire rest of my life*, she was talking to me again. Well, yee-haw.

She checked the caller ID. "It's Francesca," she announced. "She obviously knows you're home, Evie."

"Who cares? So what. Let her call all day!"

"She'd better not," Grace warned. "I have a tutor coming over this morning, and I do *not* want the phone ringing nonstop."

"Well, I can't control what Francesca does, so don't ask me," I snapped. Then I got up and ran upstairs. I put on my orange pumpkin sweater and some jeans, brushed my teeth, and called out, "BYE, I'M GOING OVER TO NISHA'S."

"So early?" Mom called from the Parent Bathroom. "Shouldn't you call first?"

"NO," I answered. "That's the last thing I should do."

I grabbed my cell and my Bubblelicious. When I got to the Guptils' my heart was pounding and I was all sweaty from running, but I banged on the door knocker without waiting to feel normal.

Mrs. Guptil opened the door, looking alarmed. "Evie, what are you doing here so early? Does Nisha know you're coming? You know she doesn't tell me anything."

"I'm sorry, she isn't expecting me, but I just really, really need to talk to her. Can I come in?"

"Yes, of course! But she's eating breakfast. And the kitchen is a disgusting mess because my housekeeper just quit." She held open the door and led me into the foyer. "Nisha my love? Your friend is here!"

"Lily?" Nisha called.

I walked into the kitchen, which looked as perfectly clean as always. Nisha was sitting at the counter, wearing penguin pj's and eating Frosted Flakes. As soon as she saw me, her mouth dropped open, and some milk dribbled down her chin.

She quickly wiped it with her sleeve. "Evie?" she said, as if she wasn't sure if I was a ghost.

"Nisha, I'm *so, so sorry*," I blurted out. "I've been the worst friend in the world. I should have talked to you. I should have listened to you. I should have—"

"Okay, Evie, slow down. So how was your date?"

I groaned.

She poured me a bowl of Frosted Flakes, and drowned it in milk. "Sit," she commanded, pointing to the stool next to her.

Then I told her the whole story. How Zane was more than half an hour late and didn't even care, how humiliated I felt when I realized he'd planned the whole thing with Francesca. Or rather, *she'd* planned the whole thing with *him*, as a setup to trick me into thinking I was having a real date. Even though it was totally obvious that Zane wanted to date Francesca and not me.

"Whoa," said Nisha when I'd finally finished. "But why are you suddenly telling me all this? Just yesterday you were, like, *mind your own business*."

"Because you were asking about something that wasn't even *my* business! I thought it was, but I was wrong. I was wrong about a *ton* of things. I was wrong about Francesca—"

"You were?"

"And you were totally right! You saw she had completely *no concept of the truth*, you tried to warn me—"

"And you didn't listen."

"Exactly."

"Because you liked her."

"Well, yes. But that was because—"

"She was fun and cool. And 'original,' right? And she was nice to you. Nicer than me, actually."

Okay, that shocked me. Because Nisha was finally apologizing: not saying the specific words "I'm sorry I've been so nasty, I'm sorry I've been so jealous," but meaning them. Which counted for a whole lot more, I realized.

I only shrugged, though, because that seemed like the right thing to do. "Whatever. We were both really upset. And, anyway, I thought you hated her."

She pushed her cereal bowl away. "I'm not a member of the Francesca Fan Club," she admitted. "But it doesn't matter, really, because *you* like her. And to be honest, listening to all this, I'm not sure what she did was so terrible."

"*What?*"

"Zane has a crush on her. Well, that's not her fault, Evie. I mean, let's face it, she's beautiful. And she has this big, big personality. So it's not surprising he would notice her."

"I'm not arguing with that!"

"Okay. But she knew how *you* felt about him. Because you told her."

"I never—"

"Fine. She knew because she's psychic." Nisha rolled her eyes. "The point is, she tried to get him to go out with *you*. She could have stolen him, she could have gone with him behind your back, but she didn't. Which makes her a good friend, not a bad one. Right?"

I thought about what she was saying. Yes, I had to admit Francesca *was* a good friend in some ways. She was loyal, she was generous, she'd tried to help me with Zane. She'd also tried to get me to work things out with my best friends. Even Nisha—who was so critical about everyone and everything—could see Francesca's good points. "But she's a terrible partner," I said aloud.

"You mean on the Attic Project?" Nisha asked. "How's that going, anyway?"

"It isn't. We basically haven't started it yet."

"You haven't *started* it? Evie, it's due on *Monday*."

"I know, I know. We're in major trouble."

"And you're not freaking out?" Nisha gave me a disbelieving smile. "You're not Evie. What have you done with Evie?"

Before I could think of some jokey answer, she pointed to my neck. "Hey. I see you're wearing that bug necklace."

"Yup."

"Even though it's gross?"

"It's *unique*," I said. "And I'm not taking it off. So get used to it, Nisha."

She stuck out her tongue at me. I stuck mine back at her. And then we both started laughing.

On the walk home half an hour later, I swished my feet in the autumn leaves. Things were basically okay with Nisha now, which meant things would be basically okay with Lily, too, as soon as I could look her in the eyes and explain. And if I couldn't explain *everything*, she'd probably understand, anyway. Because the three of us really knew one another, including all our Pros and Cons. Our friendship wasn't perfect, obviously, and a lot had happened lately. But I thought about my bug necklace, how the gross mosquito part gave the amber part *character.* So maybe LilyEvieNisha was like that, too: beautiful, but with mosquito parts.

I took a giant breath of the damp, chilly air and felt semi-normal for the first time in weeks.

Then my phone rang.

i, Evie. Where are you?"

"Francesca? How did you get my cell number?"

"I called your house. Grace gave it to me. Why, is that a problem?"

"No." I sighed. "I'm not even mad anymore."

"You mean you *were* mad? What about?"

"You don't know? The date business! The way you tricked me."

"Oh, Evie. I didn't *trick* you. I only—"

"Wanted to help. I know, Francesca. But you really,

really shouldn't have. It wasn't being honest. And you aren't my fairy godmother."

"You're right. Sorrysorrysorry."

"Besides, Zane has feelings too."

"Of course." She paused awkwardly. "He's really kind of a dolt."

"I know."

"Stunningly gorgeous, but a bloody dolt."

"*Okay.*"

"Anyway. As long as you're over him." Suddenly her voice brightened. "So here's why I'm calling: Guess what arrived the other day. Angelica's *diary.*"

"What?" I stopped walking. "What do you mean, *the other day*? When did you get it?"

"Oh, I don't remember. Wednesday, maybe."

"Wednesday? You've had it since *Wednesday*? Why didn't you tell me?"

"Well, I knew how focused you were on your date."

"Gah. Francesca. It wasn't even a date!"

"Whatever it was. You were so happy about it. So I didn't want to bother you with silly Angelica Beaumont."

"Are you crazy? I *wanted* to be bothered with Angelica

Beaumont!" I'd been shouting, so I lowered my voice. "Do you realize how far behind we are? The project is due on Monday!"

"I know," she said patiently. "That's why I'm calling. To set up some time this weekend to work on it."

I forced myself to take a long, deep breath. "Listen, Francesca. We need more than 'some time' for this project. How about right now?"

"I guess," she said doubtfully. "But Aunt Sam is still in bed. She had a big party here last night, and she's sleeping it off."

Then she hung up without saying good-bye.

I called my house to say I'd be going to the Pattisons' and raced across the entire subdivision.

Francesca greeted me in a New York Yankees sweat-shirt. "Let's go in the living room. But remember, Aunt Sam—"

"I'll be quiet," I swore. "Don't worry, I'm good at that."

The living room was a disaster. Wineglasses, guacamole, lipstick-smeared napkins, all of it left over from last night, obviously. I watched Francesca sweep a bunch of crumbs off the rabbit-furry sofa. They scattered all over the rug, and she didn't even seem to notice.

"Sorry about the mess," she said, flopping down on a squooshy sofa pillow. "Aunt Sam threw a last-minute party for Tristan Royce."

"Tristan Royce? I thought she hated him."

"Oh no, they've reconnected. Which is really so tragic, now that he's moving to L.A. to star in a sitcom. Isn't that thrilling, though? Don't you wish Aunt Sam could get a job like that?"

I shrugged. "If it's what she wants."

"Oh, I *know* it is. Anyway," she said, smiling sweetly, "Grace said you were at Nisha's. I was so thrilled. Does that mean you two are friends again?"

"Forget about Nisha!" I exploded. "Forget about Tristan Royce and his stupid sitcom! Just *please* show me this diary, *okay*?"

"Of course. But try to keep your voice down, Evie." She got up and left the living room. One of the rabbits—Tourmaline?—scampered by the sofa, twitched her pink nose at me, and scampered away.

A minute later, Francesca was back. "Here," she said, and handed me a small red book bound in leather.

I opened it.

The pages were lined, and gave off a scent like wet dust.

<u>Wednesday, April 4, 1906</u>

Blue silk frock, white sash, opal earrings.

What a glorious afternoon! Walk in the Park with Amelia (white blouse, green skirt, a bit tattered at hem, I think). Later, Tea with Mama (burgundy dress, pearls) and Cousin Letty (gray monstrosity, chipped abalone Button). Mama reports that next month the Rayburns will be having a Spring Social. I do wonder if Thomas will attend!

<u>Friday, April 6, 1906</u>

Yellow shirtwaist, v. flattering at bodice. Mother-of-pearl necklace. White linen handkerchief.

Thomas will attend! Amelia (lavender dress, horrid) says her aunt Matilda told her. I must begin planning Topics to Discuss. Perhaps I shall read the <u>San Francisco Examiner</u> in preparation. If I find the time.

<u>Monday, April 9, 1906</u>

Rose frock (perfect for complexion), garnet earrings. New silk shoes, a bit tight in toes.

Calamity! Mama (blue satin) says we are to visit with Aunt Josephine in Citrus Heights all next week! At least we will return in time for the Social, but how will I bear being bored in that stuffy old House, miles from beloved Thomas? I do wish I could remain in the City with dearest Amelia, but Mama says this is not my Choice. She is so beastly Tyrannical sometimes.

Saturday, April 14, 1906

Pink silk, single gold strand at throat, ruby earrings.

Mama (gray traveling suit, new hat I despise) and I have arrived in Citrus Heights. Aunt Josephine's house smells like soup. Oh, if only for news of Thomas! Does he notice I am Gone? Will he Forget about me in the Coming Days? A thought too dreadful to imagine!

Friday, April 20, 1906

Back in the City our Beautiful House had the most dreadful shock on Wednesday, but fortunately many of our most precious Things have survived. Mama says the City has suffered a Terrible Earthquake, which is truly so tragic for those poor, poor souls affected. Unhappily, we will be forced to remain in Citrus Heights for the Foreseeable Future. But I am hopeful, for I may see Thomas soon, as his Uncle lives not far from here, and Mama says the City is Uninhabitable at Present.

I looked up at her. I swallowed. "Francesca? Did you read this?"

She nodded.

"The whole thing?"

"Yeah."

"And does it ever get different? Does she say anything about the actual earthquake?"

"Not . . . really."

"Or the destruction? Or the evacuations? Or the looting?"

"Just what you read."

"Francesca. Eighty percent of the city was destroyed. *Eighty percent.* And all she's writing about is this jerk *Thomas*?"

"I know. It's so . . . disappointing." She sighed. "But, Evie, it's not her fault she wasn't *in* San Francisco that specific day."

"I'm not saying it's her fault! But did she at least *notice* the other people? The ones who actually suffered?"

"Not really. There's a lot more stuff about Amelia and her ugly clothes—"

"What about the swinging chandeliers?" I reread the passage about the *dreadful shock.* "Didn't you say—"

"I know! I must have heard it all wrong from Uncle Teddy.

Or maybe I just imagined it. You know how sometimes you have a memory, at least you *think* it's a memory, but maybe it's just something you've thought about over and over?" Her face crumpled up.

I shook my head. "You should have read the diary, Francesca. Before you told me what it said."

"You're right. You're absolutely right! I feel so—"

"Okay," I interrupted. "Anyway, it's my fault too."

She looked up at me. "It is?"

"Yeah." I sighed. "I should have been more focused."

"Oh, but you *were*, Evie! You read all those massive books!"

"Well, I should've made sure we had the *diary*. So we'd have known all this stuff weeks ago. Before it was too late." Because what an idiot I'd been, wasting all this time, obsessing about all the wrong things. Like Espee's computer screen. And Samantha's locket. And of course my non-date with Zane. I flipped helplessly through the book. Gorgeous, perfectly written words caught my eyes: *Dance. Chocolate. True love.* "Anyway, I thought Angelica was supposed to be this big suffragette. And an artist."

"She was! I guess that was later. In 1906 she was just a teenager."

"And a spoiled, boy-crazy, fashionista airhead."

Francesca shrugged.

"Okay," I said finally. "Well, I guess we have no choice. We'd better tell Espee on Monday."

"We can't!" Francesca wailed. "Because then we'll fail the class!"

"No we won't. It's just one project. I mean, we'll get a bad grade for the quarter but we'll probably pass. You've passed all your tests and homework so far, right?"

"Not . . . exactly. I was sort of counting on the Attic Project to even things out."

I stared at her. "You were basing your entire grade on a diary you'd never even *read*? Are you crazy?"

All of a sudden Francesca burst into tears. "I can't fail Spush! Daddy said he was giving me one more chance and then shipping me off to Aunt Beebee's. I *can't* go there, Evie! She hates my mother! Her house is nothing but giant TVs all over the place, and she lives on Lean Cuisine!"

By now I was used to being shocked by Francesca, but somehow the sight of her crying really shook me up. I mean, I knew that her life was sort of a disaster, actually, with her parents on different continents and the aunts fighting on the phone every night. And I could definitely see why she'd hate living with someone who said things like *That's life for you, girls. One snag after another.* But despite all that, it was as if it had never occurred to me before that Francesca *could* cry. It just wasn't my picture of her, somehow.

"Okay," I said, watching her wipe her eyes with a crumpled tissue she'd had in her pocket. "Well, what do you suggest we do, then? We can't analyze the diary. There's nothing to analyze."

"I know." She sniffed. Her nostrils were all pink now, like a rabbit's. "Maybe we could elaborate."

"What?"

"Well, you did all that research, right? Maybe we could just . . ." She honked her nose. "Add in some detail."

"Add it *in*?"

"Nothing untrue. Just a few historical facts. From, you know, U.S. history."

I stared. "You mean you want us to pretend she wrote in her diary about the San Francisco Earthquake?"

"Well, just for the sake of this assignment. Like Espee did, when she wrote that fake love letter for the Mystery Box."

Now I laughed, but only because I didn't know what else to do. "Are you insane? You think what Espee did is the same thing as us inventing a document to pretend to analyze?"

"I truly don't see the difference, Evie." Francesca smiled hopefully. "And besides, doesn't Espee always say you can learn history from stories?"

I stood up. "No. That's not what she means, Francesca. She just means history is all the stuff that *happens* to people. Or what they *think* happens to them, which is totally different from lying." I held up the diary. "Okay if I take this with me?"

"Well, sure," she said uncertainly. "But does that mean you're going now? I thought you said we're so behind. And that we needed to work all weekend!"

"Right," I said. "We definitely do. But now I really just need to think."

chapter 24

hen I walked into the kitchen, Grace was sitting at the table with her SAT tutor. "Draw the strongest inference possible," he was telling her.

"Grace? Can I talk to you a second?" I begged.

She looked up at me as if I'd just asked to borrow her bra.

"Okay, I mean later?" I said. "When you're done?"

"When I'm *done*," she agreed.

I went upstairs to my room. I sat on my bed and opened the diary.

June 21, 1906
    Lavender shirtwaist. For luncheon today Lemon Tart, which I Merely Nibbled, as I am desperate for Thomas to admire my Green Dress.

Gah. The girl was hopeless, but I refused to lie about what she wrote. I just wouldn't—not even to save Francesca from Aunt Yellowteeth. But if we didn't lie, and if we couldn't just tell Espee the truth, what exactly were our options here?

I switched on my computer. Then I typed:

April 18, 1906, was a day Angelica Beaumont would never forget. Although she was ? miles from San Francisco, safe and sound in a dreary suburb, her life was deeply affected by the quaking earth, although in *extremely* subtle ways.

I hit the delete key. Because of course that was total garbage.

About fifteen minutes later Grace walked into my bedroom. "So?" she demanded. "What's the big emergency?"

"Could you please sit down?" I begged. "It's kind of a long story."

I told her everything. She was such a brilliant student, I figured that if anyone would know what to do, it would be Grace. And the amazing thing was, she listened really hard the whole time, never once giving me her superior smile or making some snotty comment about how irrelevant my problem was because I was *only in seventh grade*.

When I was done, she pursed her lips. "Here's my personal advice," she said. "Read the assignment."

"What?"

"I'm serious. *Read the assignment.* Try to figure out what Espee is actually asking.".

"I've already read the dumb assignment, Grace!"

"Then I don't think you *understand* it, Evie. Give me the assignment sheet."

I fished it out of my backpack and handed it to her. She frowned at it, then pointed to the middle of the page:

Step 3: Analyze closely, using multiple outside sources. (Take lots of notes. Try to fill a whole spiral notebook!)
Step 4: Find out all you can about the author. What sort of storyteller is/was he/she?

Grace started to do her smile at me. "All right, Evie. *Now* do you see what she wants you to do?"

"Noooo."

"So think harder."

I laughed desperately. "I'm supposed to write an essay about what a horrible storyteller Angelica Beaumont was?"

"Exactly," she answered. "By showing how much she missed."

I ran over to Grace and gave her a big hug. She was a little surprised by that, but even sort of hugged me back.

"Just try not to type so loud," she teased. "I've got a ton of work."

"Well, so do I," I said, sticking out my tongue.

Then I sat down at my computer.

I worked all afternoon, and after supper, and almost the entire Sunday. When it was done it was twelve typed pages (minus the bibliography), the longest essay I'd ever written. I was especially proud of the introduction:

On Wednesday, April 18, 1906, the earth shook, but not for everyone.

In San Francisco, an earthquake measuring 8.3 on the Richter scale rocked the streets. More than 80 percent of the city was destroyed, both from the quake and the fires that followed. Approximately 3,000 people were killed, and approximately 300,000 people were left homeless. Many of these were poor people forced to live in makeshift tents on the beaches and in Golden Gate Park. It was a catastrophe even worse than Hurricane Katrina.

Some people, especially the very rich, fled the city and quickly resumed a "normal" life in suburbs miles from San Francisco. One such person was sixteen-year-old Angelica Beaumont, who was so focused on her love life and all the superficial details of her boring existence that she barely registered the (as she put it) "dreadful shock."

As soon as the whole thing was printed out, I brought it over to Francesca's house and rang the doorbell. No one answered, so I stood there in the cold wind, listening to the obnoxious Big Ben chime. Finally I heard some scuffling in the entry. "Topaz, you naughty little imp!" Samantha was shouting. At last she opened the door and beamed at me. "Evie. What a lovely surprise. I hope you're not here for Frankie."

"Why not?"

"Because she isn't here." She made this graceful sort of won't-you-come-in movement with her arm, and the next thing I knew I was in her living room, which had been vacuumed and aired out, even though the sofa was still full of rabbit fur.

"Please have a seat," she said sweetly. "Would you like a latte? I have a new machine." She waved toward the kitchen.

"No thanks. Um, where is Francesca, exactly? Because we're working on this project—"

Samantha held up a perfectly manicured hand. "Frankie is off to the beach house with Mimi. As of seven this morning."

"The beach house? But it's freezing out."

"I know. Not my choice for a getaway, but try telling that to Mimi. Especially when she blows in here to rescue her daughter."

"From what?"

"Who knows. Frankie called Paris Saturday morning and said she needed rescuing. She was crying so much, it was hard to understand. Something about a basement or a cellar."

"You mean an attic?"

"Yes, that's right. An attic. And she kept saying what a dreadful friend she was, and how she'd let you down. Anyway, she finally convinced Mimi, who took the first flight out of Paris and whisked Francesca off to the beach house. *In my car.*"

"I'm sorry."

"What for? *You* didn't steal my car!"

"I know. I'm just . . ." I had no idea what to say next, so I stood up. "Do you know when Frankie will be back?"

"Impossible to say. Maybe they'll stay there forever, for all I know! Mimi gets these wild impulses—" She fluttered her hand. "On the other hand, my sister gets bored very easily. So they could be back in a week or two. I really haven't the faintest idea what's going on."

I put the Attic Project on the coffee table. "Well, when you see her, can you give this to her? We worked on it together."

"You mean for school?" She sighed sharply. "Oh, yes,

school. And I'm supposed to tell them something about Frankie's whereabouts, I suppose. Well, what do you suggest I say?"

"I don't really—"

"Wait right there." She stood up from the sofa and floated up the stairs. A minute later she returned and handed me some stationery. I immediately recognized the pale green Trident color and the <SP> monogram.

This is what she'd written:

To Whom It May Concern,

Francesca Pattison will regretfully be unable to attend Blanton Middle School for the next week or so, due to family.

Warmest wishes,
Samantha Pattison

She read it over my shoulder. "Do you think that will do?"

"I'm sure it's fine," I said seriously.

"Well, then, can I ask you an enormous favor, sugarpie? Could you possibly hand it to someone over there for me? I'd pop by myself, but I've got a huge audition tomorrow."

"No problem." Just then one of the rabbits scampered past my feet and almost threw me off balance. But I didn't fall. "Well, see you."

"Eventually," she said, waving good-bye.

he next morning I went to school early so I could slip Samantha's note in Espee's mailbox. (Don't ask me why; I guess I just thought that if any teacher on the Hard Team could deal with it, it would be Espee.) As soon as I got to Morning Homeroom, Lily ran over and gave me a big hug. "I'm so glad you talked to Nisha," she told me. "That was really, really important, Evie."

"Then you're not mad at me anymore?"

"I was never really mad to begin with," she said sweetly.

I could have answered something like, *Well then, why weren't you talking to me?* But by now all I wanted was for the weirdness to end. So I kept my mouth shut and smiled back at her.

And then magically, everything was normal again. I sat with Nisha and Lily at lunch and we spent the period giggling about Can You Please Pass the Syrup. They didn't ask very much about Francesca, and I really didn't want to talk about her. And it wasn't only because I was still keeping a lot of that sort of private. I also just needed a break from everything Francesca-related, to be honest.

The day went by quietly. I didn't even see Theo talking to Espee in the hall. And then, in Spush, the Attic Projects were due.

I handed in ours, along with the diary, exactly the way Espee told us to. For a title I'd written "ANGELICA BEAUMONT'S EARTHQUAKE." And under that I'd written "BY EVA JANE WEBBER AND FRANCESCA PATTISON," even though Francesca had done basically zero work.

Then, like everybody else on the Hard Team, I waited nervously to get it back.

Three days later, Espee walked slowly into the classroom carrying a big cardboard box, which she carefully put down on her desk. "All right," she said. "I have your Attic Projects to return to you, but first let me explain my system. I don't believe in writing directly on your work, because I think it's disrespectful. So I'm giving you my comments in a sealed envelope addressed to both members of the team. I hope you'll open your envelopes in private, and not discuss my comments with anyone but me. Any questions?"

No one was stupid enough to raise their hand. So then she started handing back everybody's project, each with a white envelope paper-clipped to the essay.

When it came time for her to hand back mine, she pressed her hand on my shoulder. "Evie, would it be okay for you to stay after class for a minute?"

My stomach flipped. "Oh sure," I said brightly.

As soon as she walked away, Nisha poked me. "Don't freak," she whispered. "It's probably just because she loved it."

I nodded because I couldn't even talk.

When class was over, everybody walked out of the room and went off somewhere to rip open their envelopes. Espee sat at her desk reading something on her computer. When we were the only two left, she closed the door and then handed me Angelica's diary, my essay, and the white envelope.

Which had a funny little bulge in it.

"I thought you should have it back now," she said quietly. "Open the envelope, Evie."

So I did.

And the locket fell onto my desk with a hollow clank.

"I'm so sorry!" I blurted out.

She cocked her head to one side. "Are you? What for?"

"I put it on your desk! It was all my stupid idea, and I know I shouldn't have done it, and I feel terrible!"

She smiled, but only just a little. "Well. I'm glad you're being honest, Evie."

"Then you're not mad?"

"Hmm. That's sort of a tricky question, actually. Let me put it this way: What I'm more upset about is the letter."

"The letter?"

"I think you know what I'm talking about. Someone sent a letter in my name to another teacher. And they had no right to do that."

I thought I'd faint. Just collapse in a blobby, boneless heap, right there on the floor. "Please don't be mad, Ms. Pierce. She was only trying to—" I stopped; I wasn't sure how to finish that sentence.

"What, Evie? What exactly *was* Francesca trying to do?"

I stared. What had just happened? I hadn't said Francesca's name, had I? But if Espee had already figured it out, did it even matter what I'd said? I swallowed hard and asked, "Then you knew Francesca sent it?"

She pursed her lips. "Not right away. When Mr. Rafferty first showed me the letter, of course I recognized what I'd written for the Civil War Mystery Box. So naturally I suspected Katie and Brendan."

"Oh, no," I said, horrified. "Katie and Brendan would never—"

"And then I got the locket, so I realized that the prank wasn't just about the Attic Project. But the letter and the locket were obviously related, so I decided to use the locket as a test."

"A . . . test?"

She nodded slowly, watching my face. "I figured whoever reacted when I wore the locket probably had something to do with the letter. And when you saw me wearing the locket, you turned bright red. So I knew you were involved, even though I couldn't see you forging the letter. But I started wondering about your partner."

Deep breaths, Evie, I said to myself.

"Then on Monday I received this absence excuse from

Francesca's aunt." She opened her desk drawer and took out Samantha's note. "And that obviously settled the question."

She put the pale green absence note on my desk. Then she reached into her leather briefcase and took out an official-looking folder. She opened the folder, held up a second sheet of pale green paper, and put it right beside the absence note. My eyes stared blindly at the identical <SP> monograms, then at the words written below: *Unable to attend. Due to family. O my darling. Cruel fate has come between us.* I'd delivered the absence note to Espee, written on the same stationery Francesca had used for the love letter. I hadn't meant to expose Francesca, but that really didn't matter now. "Is she in trouble?" I asked softly.

"Well, sure she is. Do you think she could forge a teacher's handwriting and *not* get in trouble?"

I couldn't answer that. Because the truth was, ever since I'd first met her, Francesca had me convinced that most rules didn't apply to her. "What's going to happen?"

"I'm not sure. That's up to the principal."

"And . . . is Mr. Rafferty mad too?"

"Well, he's not happy. But I have to tell you, Evie, I'm a little more upset than he is. Maybe because Francesca used *my* words and *my name*."

Her voice wobbled, and suddenly I understood that she'd been fighting with Theo about this. That's what I'd overheard in front of the main office, when she'd told him, *Don't tell me how I'm supposed to feel.* And could this also have been what they'd been fighting about in the parking lot? It was too much to even think about.

My throat was starting to ache now. "Ms. Pierce, *please* don't blame everything on Francesca. I was the one who read your computer. And I told Francesca about it, but that was before we knew he was married!"

Espee crossed her arms. Her face was pale and her aquamarine eyes looked dark. "Evie, *you* read my computer?"

I nodded.

"That's a violation of my privacy. I'm surprised. I never thought you'd do something like that."

"I know!" I said, my voice croaking. "I completely messed up! I've just been acting weird lately, I don't know what's wrong with me, but it's like I got all carried away and my brain turned off. But it's back on now, I'll never do any of this again, and I'm just really, really sorry."

The words *really, really sorry* stayed in the air for a few seconds, like the way fireworks shimmer in the sky before they disappear. And if I could have kept them up there a little longer, I would have. Because truthfully, seeing that disappointed look in her eyes, I'd never been sorrier in my life.

Espee sat down in Nisha's chair. Her hair swung forward, and she tucked it behind her ears. "Listen to me," she said quietly. "Every single person in the world has a unique story. In a way, that's all we have. And one person's story isn't better than anyone else's. Or more real."

"I know that."

"Do you? Because everything that happened here—the letter and the locket—makes me wonder if you've been trying to write my story. Which no one has a right to do but me."

I nodded blindly. Espee pressed my shoulder with her cool, dry hand. "All right, Evie, never mind about Francesca. Why don't we talk about Angelica."

My head was spinning. "Angelica?"

"Why? Is that surprising?"

"Well, no, except there really isn't much to talk about. I mean, her diary is just so . . . empty."

"You think so? You know, Angelica Beaumont grew up to be a compassionate, creative, powerful woman."

"I heard. Francesca told me. But—"

"Which leads me to wonder if some of those same impulses were apparent in her diary. Beneath the surface."

I thought about that for three seconds. "I don't think so. I mean, Ms. Pierce: All this *stuff* was going on around her, and all she did was obsess about her own dumb little world. And about a stupid crush that was probably based on nothing."

Espee's eyes sparkled. "So at age sixteen she was in a bit of a rut?"

"What?"

I could see her crooked teeth. When she smiled like that, she looked about eight years old, the way she did in that photo. "The point I'm trying to make," she said, "is that you were pretty hard on Angelica in your essay. And I know it's tempting to think you can tell someone's whole story just by looking at them in one light. But you can't. People are complicated. And everybody's story has many chapters."

She stood up. "You'd better go now. Do you want me to send the locket home to Francesca?"

I suddenly realized that if she did that, Samantha would know we'd stolen it. And Francesca was already in enough trouble. "No, that's okay," I said quickly. "I'll give it to her myself."

Then she went back to her computer and started typing something, so I stuffed the locket and the diary into my backpack and left the room, holding my essay and my envelope. As soon as I was out in the hall, I ripped open the envelope.

Espee had given us a B+. Not the best grade in the world, but not the worst, either.

Underneath the grade, this is what she'd written:

A very challenging storyteller, and a very challenging story. I hope you enjoyed the process of trying to see the world through someone else's eyes—which, in the end, is what this project was all about.
—S.P.

chapter 26

That night I was clicking aimlessly around Theo's website, thinking maybe he'd posted an up-to-the-minute photo: *The Artist and His Beloved Family*, or *A Dog Is Forev*. And all of a sudden, there was a window on my screen. An IM to *eveningstar* from someone named scalawag.

Scalawag?

"Hi, Evie," it said.

I immediately typed back: Who is this?

Scalawag answered: Quentin. Frankie's cousin? Remember me, thou miserable wench?

I had to laugh. I typed back: Sure I do, scurvy dog. How did U get my screenname?

scalawag: How do U think? Frankie.

eveningstar: Right. Stupid me. Speaking of her, what's going on? Have you talked to her?

scalawag: Yeah. Couple of times.

eveningstar: Is she coming back here?

scalawag: IDK. Aunts are duking it out right now. Big family melee.

eveningstar: 2 bad. Tell her I'm not still mad, OK? Tell her I turned in the project.

scalawag: What project? You mean the one about Angelica?

eveningstar: Yeah. Can't believe you remembered.

scalawag: Yarrr. I forget nothing, rascally knave. Maybe I can read it sometime?

eveningstar:

scalawag: Evie? U still there?

eveningstar: Yes . . . um, Quentin? Do you ever visit Blanton?

scalawag: Sure. Sometimes.

eveningstar: Next time you do, want to go to the

movies with me? We'll have to invite like 10 other people, but . . .

scalawag: Cool. Yeah. That would be great.

eveningstar: OK. Well, B4N!!!

I logged off. *Well, yee-haw,* I whispered to myself, grinning.

A few days later, I still hadn't heard anything from Francesca and was starting to think that maybe she was gone for good. Because hadn't she said that her mom loved the beach house? And that she personally wished she could stay there forever? I imagined the two of them taking long walks on the beach, finding clamshells in the sand and discussing cosmos questions under the stars. And Francesca so happy to be reunited with Mother Darling that she wasn't even wearing her sparkly blue stilettos.

Besides, I asked myself, why should Francesca *want* to come back to Blanton? Especially if she had the chance to stay at the beach house, or possibly fly off with Mimi to Paris. I wondered if Samantha Pattison would walk across the yard to tell me if Francesca had left for good. And of course Samantha was never home after school, so I couldn't just ring the Big Ben doorbell and ask.

That Saturday afternoon, Nisha and Lily were hanging out in my bedroom. Grace, miraculously, had gone off to the movies with a bunch of friends, so for once we could make as much noise as we liked. Which was a really good thing, because Lily's cousin had given her a ton more magazines, and we were laughing our heads off as we took the dorky personality quizzes.

"Here's one for Evie," Nisha said. "'You've just discovered that your BF is a brainless, two-timing loser. Do you (a) Keep it to yourself, even if that causes indigestion; (b) text, like, practically everyone in existence; (c) Confide only in your nearest and dearest—'"

"Let me see that," I said, snatching the magazine from Nisha. Just as my eyes were focusing on the tiny print, the doorbell rang.

"Shouldn't you answer it?" Lily asked, reading over my shoulder.

"Nope. Mom's in the kitchen; she'll get it. Oh great, you guys. Now I've lost my place."

"'Nearest and dearest,'" Nisha said, pointing.

"Right. Here we go. 'Nearest and dearest. Or (d) Toss a water balloon in his face.'"

Lily grabbed the magazine. "It *says* that?"

Nisha laughed. "Of course not, Lily! That's just Evie being *mature*."

"I *am* mature," I said, sticking out my tongue. "More mature than you think."

"What's that supposed to mean?" Nisha demanded.

"Oh, nothing."

There was a knock on my door. We looked at each other.

The door opened slightly. "Evie?" Francesca said.

I ran over to hug her. She smelled sharp and salty, like the ocean. "Omigod," I cried, "I'm so glad to see you! When did you get back?"

"I don't know. Maybe ten minutes ago."

"With Mimi?"

"Yeah. But she just left for the airport. Aunt Sam's giving her a lift."

"Already?"

She shrugged.

"And you're okay?"

"I'm fine. Just so bloody relieved to be back!"

I looked at her face. Her eyes seemed pale and tired, as if she hadn't been sleeping a whole lot lately. And her golden tan was completely gone by now, so you could see she had pale freckles on her cheeks. Or maybe she'd always had them, and I'd just never noticed before. Or maybe I'd just been looking at her in a single kind of light.

"So," I said quietly, "have you heard anything from school?"

"You mean from the principal?" She scrunched her forehead. "Sadly, yes. So has Mimi. And Daddy, I'm afraid."

"Does that mean you're getting—"

"No, no, I'm not expelled. And Daddy was merciful, so I'm spared Aunt Beebee. But she's ready to pounce, so of course now I'll have to be on my absolute most perfect behavior."

Behind me, I could hear Nisha give a little disbelieving sniff.

Francesca peeked over my shoulder. "Anyway," she said cheerfully, "what's been going on?"

"Not much," Lily answered politely. "We're just, you know. Hanging out."

"Oh," Francesca said. "Sounds like fun."

There was a weird pause.

"Hey, we got back our Attic Project," I said. "We did great."

"We did?" Francesca's face lit up. "Oh, Evie, we should celebrate!"

"How?"

"I'm not sure. Wait, I just had an absolutely *epic* idea: Why don't we all go to I Scream and get big embarrassing sundaes? My treat." She reached into her jeans pocket and pulled out two crisp twenty-dollar bills. Something told me the money was from Mimi, as a parting gift.

"That sounds perfect," I said.

"I don't know," Nisha said slowly. She glanced at Lily.

"Why not?"

"Well for one thing, Evie, it's too cold for ice cream."

"There aren't any rules when it comes to ice cream," I said firmly. "Besides, if I'm going to see Zane, I need my best friends with me. And that means you."

Nisha sighed. Then she nodded. "All right," she said. "Sure."

Lily smiled at me. "Okay if I check on Jimmy first? It's on the way."

"Who's Jimmy?" Francesca asked eagerly.

"A hairy old guy with a smell issue," Nisha said.

"Lily's dog," I explained. "A real sweetheart."

"Oh, lovely, I absolutely *adore* old dogs," Francesca cried. She did that heart-attack thing. "Old dogs are like poets, don't you think? They have such deep, deep souls."

Nisha gave me a look like, *Please tell me she didn't say that*. But I just grinned back at her and shrugged. It was hard to imagine LilyNishaEvieFrancesca, but who knew, maybe it could work. And now we'd be going out for big, embarrassing sundaes. That was definitely a start.

I grabbed my cell phone and my Bubblelicious, and checked to make sure my amber necklace was clasped tightly around my neck. Then all four of us ran down the steps and out the door into the freezing sunshine.

Tales from a
NOT-SO-
Fabulous Life

She's a self-proclaimed dork. She
has the coolest pen ever. She keeps
a top-secret diary.
Read it if you dare.

By Rachel Renée Russell

From Aladdin
Published by Simon & Schuster

FIVE GIRLS. ONE ACADEMY. AND SOME SERIOUS ATTITUDE.

CANTERWOOD CREST

by Jessica Burkhart

TAKE THE REINS

CHASING BLUE

BEHIND THE BIT

TRIPLE FAULT

BEST ENEMIES

LITTLE WHITE LIES

RIVAL REVENGE

HOME SWEET DRAMA

Don't forget to check out the website for
downloadables, quizzes, author vlogs, and more!
www.canterwoodcrest.com

FROM ALADDIN M!X   PUBLISHED BY SIMON & SCHUSTER

Barbara Dee knows what tweens like!
Collect every one of her M!X books.

Just Another Day
in My Insanely Real Life

Solving Zoe

This Is Me From Now On

From Aladdin · Published by Simon & Schuster